AROUND CHI-TOWN

As the trumpeters blare in the Grand Cathedral halfway around the world, our own Daniel Connelly is about to become crowned king of Altaria. Plans are under way for the coronation, set to take place right after Christmas. All of Chicago's own royal family, the Connellys, reportedly will be there for the event.

Including the latest Connelly in the news—Maggie. The youngest Connelly has recently made a splash of her own in the tabloids. Reckless, impetuous Maggie has been seen around town and in—shall we say?—compromising positions with the P.I. on the Connelly case—hard-boiled Cherokee Lucas Starwind. A surprise? Not really. Chicago has come to expect the outrageous from young Maggie.

But trouble still rages for our most beloved family. The professional hit man arrested last month confessed he had the Connellys in his sights and allegedly detailed an organized-crime smuggling ring targeting the billion-dollar Connelly Corporation. Police are keeping the details close to the vest.

As Christmas approaches, the paparazzi—including yours truly—will flock to Altaria for the elaborate coronation. The eyes of Chicago will be watching closely, as there is one hit man still at large.....

D1044607

Dear Reader,

'Tis the season to read six passionate, powerful and provocative love stories from Silhouette Desire!

Savor *A Cowboy & a Gentleman* (#1477), December's MAN OF THE MONTH, by beloved author Ann Major. A lonesome cowboy rekindles an old flame in this final title of our MAN OF THE MONTH promotion. MAN OF THE MONTH has had a memorable fourteen-year run and now it's time to make room for other exciting innovations, such as DYNASTIES: THE BARONES, a Boston-based Romeo-and-Juliet continuity with a happy ending, which launches next month, and——starting in June 2003—Desire's three-book sequel to Silhouette's out-of-series continuity THE LONE STAR COUNTRY CLUB. Desire's popular TEXAS CATTLEMAN'S CLUB continuity also returns in 2003, beginning in November.

This month DYNASTIES: THE CONNELLYS concludes with *Cherokee Marriage Dare* (#1478) by Sheri WhiteFeather, a riveting tale featuring a former Green Beret who rescues the youngest Connelly daughter from kidnappers. Award-winning, bestselling romance novelist Rochelle Alers debuts in Desire with *A Younger Man* (#1479), the compelling story of a widow's sensual renaissance. Barbara McCauley's *Royally Pregnant* (#1480) offers a fabulous finale to Silhouette's cross-line CROWN AND GLORY series, while a feisty rancher corrals the sexy cowboy-next-door in *Her Texas Temptation* (#1481) by Shirley Rogers. And a blizzard forces a lone wolf to deliver his hometown sweetheart's infant in *Baby & the Beast* (#1482) by Laura Wright.

Here's hoping you find all six of these supersensual Silhouette Desire titles in your Christmas stocking.

Enjoy!

Joan Marlow Golan

Joan Marlow Golan
Senior Editor, Silhouette Desire

Please address questions and book requests to:
Silhouette Reader Service
U.S.: 3010 Walden Ave., P.O. Box 1325, Buffalo, NY 14269
Canadian: P.O. Box 609, Fort Erie, Ont. L2A 5X3

Cherokee
Marriage Dare
SHERI WHITEFEATHER

Published by Silhouette Books

America's Publisher of Contemporary Romance

Special thanks and acknowledgment are given
to Sheri WhiteFeather for her contribution to the
DYNASTIES: THE CONNELLYS series.

To the editors on this series, thank you for your
hard work and dedication. And to the other authors who
made the Connelly family come alive—your emotional
and creative support was truly appreciated.

 SILHOUETTE BOOKS

ISBN 0-373-76478-2

CHEROKEE MARRIAGE DARE

Copyright © 2002 by Harlequin Books S.A.

Visit Silhouette at www.eHarlequin.com

Printed in U.S.A.

Books by Sheri WhiteFeather

Silhouette Desire

Warrior's Baby #1248
Skyler Hawk: Lone Brave #1272
Jesse Hawk: Brave Father #1278
Cheyenne Dad #1300
Night Wind's Woman #1332
Tycoon Warrior #1364
Cherokee #1376
Comanche Vow #1388
Cherokee Marriage Dare #1478

SHERI WHITEFEATHER

lives in Southern California and enjoys ethnic dining, summer powwows, and visiting art galleries and vintage clothing stores near the beach. Since her one true passion is writing, she is thrilled to be a part of the Silhouette Desire line. When she isn't writing, she often reads until the wee hours of the morning.

Sheri also works as a leather artisan with her Muscogee Creek husband. They have a son, a daughter and a menagerie of pets, including a pampered English bulldog and four equally spoiled Bengal cats. She would love to hear from her readers. You may write to her at: P.O. Box 5130, Orange, California 92863-5130.

MEET THE CONNELLYS

Meet the Connellys of Chicago—
wealthy, powerful and rocked by scandal,
betrayal...and passion!

Who's Who in
CHEROKEE MARRIAGE DARE

Lucas Starwind—His new "partner" on the case is an
innocent who needs protection...and is a woman who
threatens his heart.

Maggie Connelly—The youngest Connelly is never taken
seriously...that is, until she embarks upon the seduction
of Luke Starwind.

Rocky Palermo—The professional killer takes pride
in his work. Nothing—and no one—keeps him from
completing a job.

One

Maggie Connelly waited on Luke Starwind's doorstep. The Chicago wind blew bitter and brisk. She could feel the December air creeping up her spine like icy fingers. A warning, she thought. A prelude to danger.

Adjusting the grocery bags in her arms, she shifted her stance. Was she getting in over her head? Playing with fire?

No, she told herself. She had every right to get involved in her family's investigation. She needed to make a difference, to find closure. Her beloved grandfather was dead, and so was her dashing, handsome uncle. Their lives had been destroyed, and she needed to know why.

But her biggest stumbling block was Luke. She knew the former Green Beret would try to thwart her efforts.

Maggie tossed her head. Well, she had a surprise in store for him. She'd uncovered a valuable piece of evidence. And that was her ace in the hole, the card up her sleeve. He couldn't very well shut her out once she revealed the winning hand fate had dealt her.

Luke opened the door, but neither said a word.

Instead, their gazes locked.

Maggie took a deep breath, forcing oxygen into her lungs.

The man stood tall and powerfully built. Jet-black hair, combed away from his forehead, intensified the rawboned angles of his face. He possessed a commanding presence, his features strong and determined—high-cut cheekbones, a nose that might have suffered a long-healed break, an unrelenting jaw.

Luke was a jigsaw puzzle she'd yet to solve, each complicated piece of his personality as confusing as the next. Everything about him rattled her senses, and made her want to touch him. Not just his body, but also his heart.

His reclusive, shielded heart.

Did Luke know that he had a romantic side? A masculine warmth hidden beneath that stern, rugged exterior?

Maggie had asked him to dance at her brother's wedding reception, and now she could feel every gliding motion, every smooth sultry sway. He'd rubbed his cheek against her temple and whispered a Cherokee phrase, something that had made him draw her closer to his beating heart. She'd never been so tenderly aroused.

"What are you doing here?"

Instantly, Maggie snapped to attention. After that sensual dance, he'd avoided her like the plague, returning to his hard-boiled self.

But why? she wondered. Because she'd made him feel too much?

Refusing to be intimidated, she shoved the groceries at him. "I came to fix you dinner, Starwind. So be a gentleman, will ya?"

Flustered, he took the bags, nearly dropping one in the process.

Maggie bit back a satisfied smile. She'd managed to catch Mr. Tough Guy off guard. That in itself rang like a small victory.

He moved away from the door, and she swept past him, curious to see his home.

The spacious, two-story town house showcased a stone fireplace and nineteenth-century furnishings, each piece sturdy and functional. A little battered, she supposed, but the rustic antiques made a personal statement. She assumed Luke had chosen them, as they suited him well.

She noticed the absence of knickknacks and lived-in clutter. Apparently Luke surrounded himself with the necessities of life, rather than objects that sparked sentiment. A person's home reflected his emotions, Maggie thought. And although Luke's town house was located in the heart of the city, it made her wonder if he'd been raised on a farm or a ranch. The oak floors were polished to a slick shine and padded with braided area rugs.

She zeroed in on the kitchen and headed toward it, knowing Luke followed. He set the groceries on a tiled counter, and she familiarized herself with his spotless appliances and practical cookware. The windowsill above the stainless-steel sink was bare, no potted plants, nothing to water or care for.

Something inside her stirred—a wave of sadness, an urge to brighten his rough-hewn world. To make Mr. Tough Guy smile.

He frowned. And for an instant she feared he'd just read her mind.

He leaned against a pantry-style cabinet, watching every move she made. Maggie unbuttoned her coat and told herself to relax. The man was a top-notch private investigator.

It was his nature to study people and make analytical assessments. Plus, she thought, releasing the breath she'd been holding, he was attracted to her.

Their bodies had brushed seductively on the dance floor; their hearts had pounded to the same erotic rhythm. *A qua da nv do.* The Cherokee words swirled in her head. What did they mean? And why had he said them with such quiet longing?

Maggie hung her coat behind a straight-back chair in the connecting dining room. Luke's gaze roamed from her cashmere sweater to the tips of her Italian boots, then back up again.

"What's going on?" he asked. "What are you up to?"

"Nothing," she responded a little too innocently. She wasn't ready to drop the bomb. First she would ply him with pasta. And a bottle of her favorite wine.

Luke crossed his arms. He wore jeans and a dark-blue sweatshirt, attire much too casual for his unyielding posture. In his left ear, a tiny sterling hoop shone bright against dark skin. The earring defined the native in him, she thought. A man who remained close to his Cherokee roots.

She unloaded the groceries and realized he intended to stay right where he was, staring at her while she prepared their meal.

"I'm surprised you know how to cook," he said.

She shot him a pointed look. "Very funny." Maggie knew how Luke perceived her. No one took her endeavors seriously.

She was the youngest child in one of the wealthiest, most powerful families in the country. Her elegant mother hailed from royalty, and her steely-eyed father had made his fortune in business, transforming a small company into a global corporation.

But Maggie had yet to earn the respect often associated

with the Connelly name. The paparazzi deemed her a spoiled, jet-setting heiress. The tabloid pictures that circulated made her seem like nothing but a party girl. It was an image she couldn't seem to shake, no matter how hard she tried.

And while Maggie's personal life was dissected in gossip columns, Luke kept a tight rein on his.

Why was he so detached? she wondered. So cautious? Why would a handsome, successful, thirty-nine-year-old choose to protect his heart?

She didn't know much about Luke, but she'd done a little digging, asking for information from anyone who knew him. And although she hadn't been able to unravel the mystery surrounding him, she'd learned a few unsettling facts. Luke had never been married or engaged. He didn't participate in meaningful relationships, and most people, including women, described him as guarded.

Maggie held his watchful gaze, searching for a flicker of happiness, a spark of joy. But his eyes seemed distant. Haunted, she thought, by undisclosed pain.

Could she make him happy? Could she hold him close and ease the tension from his brow?

Deep down, she wanted the chance to try. But she doubted he would welcome her efforts. Especially when she told him that she intended to help him with her family's investigation.

Lucas Starwind, she knew, wouldn't appreciate the Connelly's youngest daughter working by his side.

A little over an hour later Luke and Maggie sat across from each other at his dining-room table. The lady was up to something. He knew she'd been questioning people all over town about him. And now here she was, enticing him with a home-cooked meal. Young, beautiful, impulsive

Maggie. The Connelly baby. The free-spirited jet-setter. Something didn't add up.

But, then, Maggie was far from predictable. She carried herself like a muse, like the goddess of dance, flaunting a playful sensuality Luke wasn't accustomed to. She wore her light-brown hair in a natural style, and her eyes were the color of a tropical sea. Long, lithe curves complemented all that unchained beauty.

She had a temper, too. Just enough to ignite his blood.

But Luke didn't like the idea that they wanted each other. She was too young for him—much too young. Seventeen years spanned between them, a lifetime in his book.

He glanced at the food she'd prepared—antipasto salad, lasagna and a loaf of oven-warmed bread. It was a cozy, charming meal. The kind of dishes a sidewalk café would serve. Even the ambience seemed intimate. Maggie had provided a scented candle, and it burned between them like a melting jewel.

But this wasn't a date, and in spite of the wine sparkling in his glass, Luke was in complete control of his senses.

Maybe not in complete control. But close. As close as his body would allow while in Maggie's presence. As long as they weren't touching, he would survive her proximity. No more dances, no more warm, gentle seductions. Luke couldn't take another bewitching. Not after what he'd said. What he'd felt.

He glanced up and caught her watching him. Waiting, he supposed, to see if this cozy dinner had affected him, if it would make him easier to deal with. He knew she was plotting something. Those blue-green eyes shimmered with what he'd come to think of as muse magic—enchantment that could steal into a man's soul.

Luke frowned, disturbed by his train of thought. Maggie

Connelly was a woman, not a muse. And he was too practical to get caught up in mythical nonsense.

Then why had she inspired him to hold her close? To sway flawlessly to the music? To whisper words he hadn't meant to say? Luke hadn't spoken the Kituwah dialect since he was a boy.

He shook his head, intent on clearing his mind. Dwelling on that moment wouldn't do him any good. He still had this other business with Maggie to contend with—whatever the hell it was.

"Level with me," he said. "Tell me what's going on."

She reached for her wine. The light from the chandelier cast an enchanting glow. Luke ignored the gilded streaks in her hair, the gold that gleamed like a treasure.

"I'm going to help you solve my family's case."

He clenched his jaw. So that was it. The grad student wanted to amuse herself by playing detective. No way, he thought. No damn way. Tom Reynolds, his experienced partner, had been killed while working on this investigation. The last thing Luke needed was an amateur sleuth—a gorgeous female—dogging his heels, getting herself into all sorts of trouble.

"This isn't a game, Maggie." He drilled her with a hard stare. "People are dying out there."

"You think I don't know that?" She bristled before her voice turned raw. "King Thomas was my grandfather. And Prince Marc was my uncle."

And both men were dead, Luke thought. Killed in a boating accident that hadn't turned out to be an accident at all. "I'm sure you're well aware that the Kelly crime family is responsible for what's been going on. And they have ties in Altaria." He leaned against the table. "This is a sophisticated operation. An international crime ring. There's someone in the royal household who's a key player in everything that happened.''

"And that's why this matters so much to me. I have a right to know why members of my family were killed. Altaria is a second home to me.''

He pictured her in Altaria, sunbathing on the white sandy beaches, strolling the cobblestoned streets, breathing in the cool, clean air. Altaria was an independent kingdom on the Tyrrhenian Sea, just off the southern coast of Italy. Yes, he thought. Maggie Connelly belonged to that world, to the picturesque island that captured the essence of her youth and royal blood. He didn't doubt that she had been King Thomas's favored grandchild.

"This case is too dangerous for sentiment.'' And he wasn't about to put her in the center of a critical investigation.

"My grandfather and my uncle are gone,'' she countered, pushing her plate away. "And I need closure.''

Luke heaved a rough sigh. If there was one thing he understood, it was the thirst for justice. But Maggie's situation was different from his. She wasn't responsible for the despair in her family. "I can't let you get involved.'' He had a darn good idea why King Thomas and Prince Marc had been killed, and the danger was still out there. A danger that threatened Mother Earth. Biological warfare wasn't child's play.

She set her chin in a defiant gesture. "I'm already involved. I have a piece of evidence, something I'm sure is related to this case.''

Silent, he studied her for a moment. Pretty Maggie— the free-spirited coed, the high-society party girl. She had to be bluffing. There was no way she could have uncovered vital information. "Really, Nancy Drew? And what might that be?''

Irked by the mockery, she met his gaze head-on, her eyes suddenly more green than blue. Like one of those mood rings, he thought with a spark of humor. The lady did have quite a temper.

"A few weeks ago I found a CD in a lace shipment from Altaria," she said, knocking the amusement right out of him. "The software is encrypted, so I couldn't read the file, but it doesn't take a genius to know that it was smuggled out of the country."

Luke's entire body tensed.

Another pirated file.

Damn it, he thought. Damn it all to hell. Maggie's discovery was enough to get her killed. "Who else have you told about this?"

"No one."

"Good." At least she had the sense to keep quiet. Unable to finish his meal, Luke set his fork back on the table. This case was tying his stomach in knots. "What were you doing nosing around at the warehouse?" She wasn't involved in the Connelly import business.

She sent him a tight look. "I wasn't nosing around. I custom ordered some lace for a dress. When it arrived, the warehouse forwarded the package to me."

A package that had accidentally contained one of the stolen files. Luke shook his head. Maggie had gotten herself tangled up in biological warfare over a dress. Somehow that made perfect, idiotic sense. "You're going to turn that CD over to me and forget that you ever saw it."

"Oh, no, I'm not. I'm keeping it until you agree to let me help you with the investigation."

She tilted her head at a regal angle, and Luke cursed beneath his breath. Women in Altaria couldn't inherit the throne, but that didn't make Maggie Connelly any less of a princess.

Her oldest brother, Daniel, had inherited the throne. Although his very public, very lavish coronation was scheduled at the end of the month, he'd already taken a private oath before the United Chambers, becoming king of the small, sovereign nation. And now King Daniel had stolen files to worry about, information that had been smuggled out of his country. He doubted the monarch would appreciate his sister withholding evidence.

Luke had the notion to wring Maggie's royal little neck. "You're not getting away with this," he said.

"And neither are you," she retorted.

Their gazes locked in a battle of wills. Luke cursed again, only this time out loud. In that long-drawn-out moment, he knew he had met his match.

And now, damn it, he had to figure out what to do about her.

The Connellys' Chicago mansion was a classic Georgian manor, located in the city's most fashionable neighborhood. The brick structure sat like a monument, surrounded by a sweeping lawn.

Luke had been escorted to a sitting room, but he didn't feel like sitting. Instead he stood beside a marble fireplace, waiting for Maggie's brother Rafe. Overall, she had eight brothers, two sisters, a graceful mother and a powerful father, but Rafe was the one Luke had been working with on the Connelly case.

Leaning against the mantel, he glanced around the room and shook his head. He couldn't imagine growing up in a place like this. Luke had found his own measure of financial success, and he appreciated antiques, but everything in the Connelly mansion was too grand for his taste.

A moment later he moved his arm, realizing it was dangerously close to what looked like a priceless vase. Ming

Dynasty, Qing Dynasty. He didn't know the difference, but knocking the damn thing over wasn't the most prudent way to find out.

Rafe entered the room, and Luke moved forward to greet him. Rafe Connelly was anything but the computer nerd Luke had expected before they'd met the first time. He was athletic and hardworking, charming when he felt like it and fond of casual clothes and fast cars. Luke respected him immensely. And if anybody could turn Maggie around, he could. Although Rafe was levelheaded, he shared a bit of Maggie's impulsive nature. Luke assumed she wouldn't resent her brother's intervention.

"Any luck?" Luke asked.

The other man shook his head. "She's upstairs in her room, hissing like a cat. There's no way she's going to relinquish that CD. Not without a compromise."

And I'm the compromise, Luke thought. Me and the investigation. "Did you tell her what's on the CD?" he asked. Rafe had recently uncovered the existence of the pirated files, as well as the lethal material they contained.

Rafe gave him an incredulous look. "Not without consulting you first."

They both fell silent, their expressions grim. They had discussed the severity of this case, the need for secrecy. Luke gazed out a French door. He could see a crop of distant shrubbery blocked in each wood-framed pane.

He turned back to Rafe. "What the hell are we going to do?"

"I don't see that we have much choice. If we don't allow Maggie to get involved, she intends to go snooping around on her own." The other man pulled a hand through his wavy light-brown hair. "I swear, I could brain her."

Luke knew the feeling. And he also knew what Rafe was getting at. Maggie was in more danger on her own than she was working by Luke's side. And her having possession of one of the CDs made it even more critical. ''I don't need this.''

''I know. I'm sorry.''

Once again they fell silent. Luke thought about Tom Reynolds, who had been shot to death while on the investigation. His stomach clenched. If he hadn't been out of town at the time, he could have given Tom the backup he needed.

''You'll have to keep a close eye on Maggie.''

He looked up and slammed straight into Rafe's dark-blue gaze. Was the other man blaming him for Tom's murder? Or was it a reflection of his own guilt he saw?

They stood in the center of the room, the finery closing in around them. Luke knew what came next. He knew exactly what Rafe was going to say.

''I'm asking you to protect my sister, Luke. To treat her as if she was your own flesh and blood.''

He locked his knees to keep them from buckling. His own flesh and blood. A pain gripped his heart. The ever-constant ache that reminded him of what he'd done. Tom Reynolds wasn't the only death he was responsible for. Twenty-seven years before, he'd let a beautiful little girl die. He would never forget the day her body had been found. The muggy summer day a farmer had discovered her, bruised and battered—tortured by a vicious attack.

''Promise me you'll protect her.''

''I will,'' Luke vowed. ''I promise.'' He would keep Rafe's sister safe. With his life, he thought. With the only honor he had left.

The other man broke the tension with a grin. ''It won't be easy. Maggie's one headstrong female.''

Luke couldn't find it within himself to smile. But he rarely could. His joy had died twenty-seven years ago.

"Yeah. I've already locked horns with her. I know what I'm up against."

"You're going to have to fill her in about what we've learned so far," Rafe said. "I don't want to give her an excuse to go poking around on her own."

Luke squinted. "Fine. But first I want you to lay some ground rules. Tell Maggie that I'm the boss. This is my investigation, and whatever I say goes."

Rafe agreed. "I'll brief her, then send her down in a few minutes."

He headed toward the French door. "Have her meet me outside. I could use some air."

"Sure. And Luke?"

He turned, his boots heavy on the Turkish carpet. "Yeah?"

"Thanks."

Luke only nodded. Protecting Maggie Connelly scared the hell out of him. But her brother had entrusted him with the responsibility. And that was something a Cherokee man couldn't deny.

Two

Maggie exited the house, then shoved her hands in her coat pockets to ward off the chill. Luke stood quietly, a lone figure surrounded by a winter garden, his face tipped to the sky.

In the distance, boxwood shrubs created a maze—a mystic castle of green. The maze was Maggie's favorite spot at Lake Shore Manor. To her, it had always seemed dark and dangerous. Haunted yet beautiful.

Like Lucas Starwind.

He wore black jeans and a leather jacket, the collar turned up for warmth. On his feet, a pair of electrician-style boots crunched on the frozen grass. As she approached, he turned to look at her.

She continued walking, and when they were face-to-face, she waited for him to speak.

But he didn't. Instead he let the wind howl between them.

Maggie had never met anyone like Luke. He had an edge,

she thought. A dark and mysterious edge, like the maze. She used to play hide-and-seek there as a child, and as much as the twists and turns had frightened her, they had thrilled her, too.

Luke, she realized, produced the same staggering effect. He looked powerful in the hazy light. His cheekbones cast a hollow shadow, and his eyes bore permanent lines at the corners. From frowning, she decided, or squinting into the sun. In his hair, she could see faint threads of gray, so faint they almost seemed like an illusion.

"Are you cold?" he asked. "Do you want to go back inside?"

She shook her head. The air was sharp and chilled, but she didn't want to break this strange spell.

"It's going to snow," he said. "By Friday. Or maybe Saturday."

The weathermen claimed otherwise, but Maggie didn't argue the point. Luke seemed connected to the elements. She attributed that to the loner in him, to the man who probably spent countless hours alone with a winter sky.

Although Maggie wanted to touch him, she kept her hands in her pockets. Luke wasn't the sort of person you placed a casual hand upon. But, then, she knew what sparked between them was far from casual.

"Did Rafe talk to you?" he asked, looking directly into her eyes.

"Yes. He said I'm supposed to listen to whatever you say." That, of course, had rubbed her the wrong way. Rafe had made her feel like a child rather than a grown woman. Then again, she had behaved badly in front of her brother, her Irish temper flaring.

"That's right. You're supposed to follow my direction, and I'm supposed to keep a close eye on you."

"Really?" Somehow that pleased and irritated her all at

once. She liked the idea of spending time with Luke, but she didn't appreciate having him as her keeper.

He lowered his chin, glaring at her through narrowed eyes. "Do you have a problem with that?"

"No." She decided she would turn his guardianship against him. She would use every opportunity she could to make him smile. To save that tortured soul of his.

"Good. Then I need some information from you."

An angry breeze blew his hair, dragging it away from his face. He had a natural widow's peak, which gave him a rather ominous appeal. Like the maze, she reminded herself. The silver earring caught a glint of the gray winter light.

"How many residences do you have?" he asked.

"Me or my family?"

"You, Maggie. Where do you sleep?"

The question had been posed in a professional voice, but there was still a note of intimacy attached. She couldn't seem to ignore the tingle it gave her.

"I have a room here," she told him. "But most of the time I stay at a loft downtown. I own the building." It was her sanctuary, her home and her studio. Maggie was an artist. She painted because she needed to, because the images she created stemmed from her emotions.

Luke shifted his stance, and she imagined painting him where he stood, the wind ravaging his hair, daylight reflecting the torment in his eyes, the silver earring catching a glint of gray from the sky.

A muscle ticked in his jaw. "Do you have a current lover? Someone who has access to your loft?"

A sensuous shiver streaked up her spine. "No." She wanted him as her lover. She wanted him thrusting inside her, clawing at her with the heat and power she knew he possessed. She met his gaze, felt her heartbeat stagger. "Do you have a current lover, Luke?"

He squinted, causing the lines around his eyes to imbed themselves deeper. "This isn't about me."

She tossed her head, but the image she'd created in her mind wouldn't go away. "So you get to pry into my life, but I have to stay out of yours?"

"That's right. And do you know why that is, Maggie?"

She didn't respond. There was no need. Clearly he intended to enlighten her.

"You're too young and too emotional," he said. "You don't observe the world through calculating eyes. You wouldn't have the slightest idea if the person following you was a cameraman or a hit man. So it's my job to know where you are and who you're with."

Counting silently to ten, and then to twenty, she suppressed the urge to fire her temper at him. "Which basically means I'm a thorn in your side."

"You're not exactly the partner I would have chosen."

Maggie saw a shadow cross his face, and she knew he was thinking about Tom Reynolds. Luke had left town for a while after his partner's funeral. He had seemed enraged at the time, barely in control of his pain.

"You're emotional, too," she said.

"Not like you. I'm not playful one minute and pissy the next."

No, she thought. He was *never* playful.

"Come on." He motioned to the courtyard, his demeanor stern and strong and businesslike. "Let's sit down, and I'll fill you in on the case."

Ten minutes later, they occupied a glass-topped table, each with a hot drink in front of them.

Maggie's mocha cappuccino tasted rich and sweet, flavored with a splash of raspberry syrup. Luke drank his coffee strong and black. Which suited him, she thought.

He lifted his gaze and looked directly into her eyes. For

an instant she held her breath. Lucas Starwind never failed to accelerate her heartbeat.

"We're dealing with the possibility of a biological weapon," he said.

The air in her lungs rushed out. "That's what's on the CD I discovered? Some sort of scientific formula that could kill people?"

He gave a tight nod. "We've recovered six CDs in all, including the one you have, but there's more out there. The files they contain were pirated from the Rosemere Institute."

"That doesn't make sense." Maggie's grandfather, King Thomas, had founded the Rosemere Institute in hopes of discovering a cure for cancer. "How could the Institute have anything dangerous in their files?"

"Because they've been focusing on viral genetic research," he explained. "The idea is to tailor a virus that will destroy cancer cells without debilitating the patient the way radiation and chemotherapy do."

Waiting for Luke to continue, Maggie placed her hands around her coffee cup, drawing warmth from the porcelain.

"Last year the Institute made a breakthrough in their research," he said. "But they also explored a number of dead ends. And one of those dead ends led to the accidental creation of a virus that stimulates a fast-growing cancer. A virus that's vectored through the air."

Momentarily stunned, Maggie stared at him. "They created a cancer? Did King Thomas know?"

"Yes. He made sure the original virus was destroyed, along with the final codes needed to fabricate it. But if a top-quality lab had all of the Institute's data, they could figure out the final codes and re-create it."

"How many of the CDs are still missing?"

"Enough to worry about. Whoever has them intends to

sell them on the black market. That's what this whole scheme is about.''

Her pulse pounded in her throat. Biological warfare wasn't what she had expected. "So this is why King Thomas and Prince Marc were killed?''

Luke paused, gauging Maggie's expression. She looked pale, sad and worried. He decided now wasn't the time to tell her that Prince Marc had most likely been involved in stealing the files. In a roundabout way, her uncle's treachery had cost him his life.

"Rafe and I aren't clear on all the details,'' he said. "We know the Kelly crime family is responsible, and even though they're in prison now, they still have ties in Altaria.''

She lifted her coffee with both hands. "So solving this case means recovering the rest of the CDs and putting the Altarian traitors behind bars?''

"That's exactly what it means.''

A moment of silence stretched between them, but Luke assumed she needed to absorb the harsh reality of what she'd just learned.

The courtyard didn't provide much of a wind block. Maggie's hair blew wildly around her shoulders, each light-brown strand tipped with gold. She wore a camel-colored coat, the collar lined with a faux-print fur. The effect was stunning. And distracting, Luke thought.

She seemed vulnerable, and that made him want to touch her.

She replaced her cup with an unsteady hand. "This is so awful. King Thomas founded the Institute because his wife died from cancer. He was trying to do something good for mankind, not destroy it. He loved his queen very much. It broke his heart to watch her suffer.''

Luke nodded. He had seen firsthand how terribly cancer patients suffered, how the disease ravaged. He had lost his father to colorectal cancer. But Luke wasn't going to tell Maggie about his past or the ache that came with it. The burden was his, and his alone. And so was the broken promise he'd made to his dad.

He stared at his coffee, into the void of nothingness. He wanted to drop his head in his hands and mourn the mistakes he'd made.

But he couldn't. There was no turning back. He had to live with what he'd done, face himself in the mirror every day and despise the reflection.

"Are you all right?" Maggie asked.

Instantly, he locked away the pain. "Of course I am."

Their eyes met and held. Hers were a pale wash of blue, flecked with tiny sparks of green. Her incredible, ever-changing eyes.

"Are you sure?" she pressed. "You seem troubled."

"It's a troubling case," he responded.

"Yes, it is," she agreed, her gaze never wavering from his.

Once again he longed to touch her. They sat side by side, their shoulders nearly brushing. He resisted the urge to lift his hand, to stroke her cheek, to feel the warmth radiating from her skin.

Luke reached for his coffee and sipped the bitter brew. This investigation was too critical to get sidetracked by a beautiful woman. Especially since she was the lady he had vowed to protect.

Rey-Star Investigations was located in a dramatic tower overlooking the city. Maggie took the elevator to the ninth floor and entered Luke's office through double-glass doors.

A blue-eyed blonde sat behind a mahogany reception desk. Focusing on a computer screen, she pursed her racy red lips, forming a provocative pout.

She was stunning—in a bombshell kind of way. A sweater, the same notice-me shade as her lipstick, stretched across her ample bosom.

Maggie frowned, irked that Luke had a blow-up doll working for him. She cleared her throat and waited for the receptionist to acknowledge her.

The blonde looked up and flashed a thousand-watt smile. That, too, managed to irritate Maggie. Apparently the other woman, who probably shared Luke's bed whenever he beckoned, didn't see her as a threat.

Clearly Luke wasn't as lonely as he appeared.

"May I help you, Ms. Connelly?" the receptionist asked.

"Yes, thank you." She wasn't surprised the other woman had recognized her. Maggie's celebrity rarely went unnoticed. "Is Mr. Starwind available?"

"I'll let him know you're here."

Within minutes Maggie was escorted into Luke's office. He stood beside a window, gazing out at the city. The room was furnished with an ebony desk, leather chairs and a lacquered bar. A slim marble table held a bronze eagle, its enormous wings poised in flight. Stone and metal, she thought, with a blend of masculine elegance.

Luke turned and met Maggie's gaze. Dressed entirely in black, he looked as striking as the decor.

He shifted his gaze to his receptionist. "Thank you, Carol."

The blonde nodded and closed the door behind her.

Luke and Maggie stared at each other for what seemed like an endless amount of time.

"She's quite the bombshell," Maggie said finally.

He moved away from the window and sat on the edge of his desk. "Who? Carol?"

Yes, Carol, she thought, wondering why he bothered to play dumb. "I wasn't aware busty blondes were your type."

He crossed his arms, his mouth set in an unforgiving line. "So you analyzed her, did you?"

"Women notice other women," she replied in her own defense. "We're quite observant in that regard."

"Really? Then why don't you give me your evaluation of her?"

Maggie removed her coat and flung it over a chair. Luke remained where he was, perched on the edge of his glossy desk.

"Let's see." She walked to the bar and poured herself a cherry cola. Rattling the ice in her glass, she took a sip. "Carol takes long lunches, wears cheap perfume and keeps her boss entertained on cold winter nights. She has an average IQ, and buys more clothes than she can afford."

Luke uncrossed his arms and tapped his chin in an analytical gesture. "That's very interesting, but you're wrong on every count. First of all, she works her tail off. Second, most perfumes, cheap or otherwise, give her a headache. She also happens to be sharp as a tack, frugal to a fault and happily married to a man who adores her."

Maggie wanted to sink into the carpet. "I suppose they have children?"

He nodded. "Two little boys. Whose pictures are prominently displayed on her desk. But you didn't notice them. Just like you didn't notice the absence of a fragrance or the gold band shining on her finger."

Mortified, she lowered herself to a chair. "I'm a lousy detective, aren't I?"

"The worst."

Maggie winced. Blond hair. Big breasts. Luke's bed. Her evaluation had stemmed from a catty scratch of jealousy. Which was something she had never experienced before.

"I'm sorry," she managed to say, thinking she owed Carol an apology as well.

SHERI WHITEFEATHER   29

He shrugged, and they both drifted into what she consid-ered uncompanionable silence. She certainly wasn't doing a very good job of making Lucas Starwind smile. And that was something she would have to remedy. Maybe not today, but soon.

"So, am I going to work with you here at the office?" she asked.

"Don't you have finals this week?"

"I can come by afterward."

"Then you're welcome to use Tom's old office."

"Thank you." She wished this wasn't a baby-sitting ef-fort on his part. Maggie preferred to earn her keep. But that rarely happened. No one gave her any credit, not even her own family.

Thoughtful, she studied her companion. Sooner or later the brooding detective would figure her out correctly. He would see her for who she really was. Wouldn't he?

"What is your type, Luke?"

He blinked. "What?"

"Your type of woman," she clarified.

He drilled her gaze, and their eyes clashed. Her pulse skipped like a stone, and she decided they were perfect for each other. No other man challenged her the way he did. Or made her care so deeply. She needed him as much as he needed her.

"I don't have one," he responded steadily.

Oh, yes you do, she thought. And I'm her.

Detective work, Maggie decided, didn't live up to its TV image. They weren't tailing bad guys, lurking in trench coats on a shadowy street corner or dodging bullets in a high-speed car chase. Instead they faced mounds and mounds of paperwork.

It was Saturday afternoon, a light snow blanketed the

ground, and she and Luke were holed up in his town house, poring over files, cataloging information about individuals and corporations known to have even the slightest association with the Kelly crime family. Luke was searching for someone, anyone, who might have an interest in the missing CDs. Locating a potential buyer, he claimed, could lead them to the Altarian traitor.

"Aren't the files encoded?" she asked. "How can they sell encrypted CDs?"

"The encryption can be broken. Not easily, but it can be done. The Kellys tried to get the encryption program from the Connelly Corporation computer system, but they failed."

"Does the Chicago P.D. know about the cancer virus? Didn't Rafe have to tell them when they arrested the Kellys?"

"No," Luke responded. "He didn't have to tell them. He led the police to believe the Kellys stole valuable data relating to the Institute's purpose—a cure for cancer. The fewer people who know the truth, the better. We don't need an international scandal on our hands."

Maggie nodded, then studied Luke's profile. He sat beside her in his home office, tapping away on a laptop.

"Why don't you send some undercover agents to Altaria?" she suggested. "There must be someone you can trust to keep an eye on things over there."

"I've already done that. I've got some former military men on it. Guys I served with. I planted someone at the castle and at the Rosemere Institute. And I've got another man watching the textile mill."

Maggie thought about the CD that had been accidentally forwarded to her. If the syndicate had discovered their error, her life would have been threatened. She understood how dangerous this case was, and she appreciated Luke for his skill and dedication. "Sounds like you've got everything under control."

"I'm trying to stay one step ahead of the game." He rolled his shoulders and nearly bumped her arm. The desk they shared was barely big enough for two. "But unfortunately the men I sent to Altaria haven't uncovered any leads."

He stopped typing and turned to look at her. His face was close enough to see the detail of his skin, the faded scar near his left eyebrow, the slight shadow of beard stubble. She was tempted to touch him, to run her fingers over those stunning cheekbones. As an artist, she was fascinated by his features. As a woman, she couldn't help but admire his rugged appeal.

"I need to tell you something about Prince Marc," he said.

Instantly Maggie braced herself. There was always something to be said about her uncle. Prince Marc had been a charming, dashing playboy. Considered one of Europe's most eligible bachelors, he'd juggled lovers the way he'd juggled his finances. He'd also fathered a daughter out of wedlock, but unfortunately hadn't proved to be much of a parent.

Nonetheless, Maggie had loved him. He was still her blood.

"Prince Marc had an association with the Kellys," Luke announced.

For a moment she only stared. Her uncle, the free-spirited prince, had been involved in organized crime? A man the media often compared her to?

Her stomach knotted. "In what capacity?"

"He owed the Kellys money. His gambling debts were eating him alive." Luke sighed. "We believe he was part of the smuggling scam, Maggie."

''That can't be.'' She jumped to her feet, paced a little. ''He was murdered in the same speedboat accident as the king. They were together.''

''Think about it. Prince Marc hadn't originally planned on being on the boat that day. He'd gone with his father at the last minute. Therefore, he wasn't the intended hit.''

She stopped pacing. ''So what's your theory?''

''Prince Marc needed to get out from under his gambling debts, so he formed an alliance with the Kellys. In fact, I think they killed King Thomas because they wanted Marc, a man they could easily manipulate, to take the throne.''

''But they accidentally killed Marc instead.'' Which meant that her uncle hadn't known that the Kellys meant to murder the king. But someone at the castle did. Someone who had kept the Kellys informed of the king's whereabouts, someone who had sent a hit man to the dock to tamper with the boat.

She blinked, fighting tears she wouldn't dare cry in front of Luke. King Thomas had been her salvation, the only person in the world who truly understood her, who knew how diligently she struggled to earn her family's respect.

Frivolous Maggie. The temperamental artist. The spoiled Connelly baby. No one seemed to care that she was earning a double major in business and art.

Damn it, she thought, missing the king's keep-your-chin-up encouragement.

She worked as hard as she played. Harder, she decided, staring at the stack of paperwork on Luke's desk. She'd studied for finals in the midst of all this. And now she had to contend with images of her traitorous uncle.

Weary, she shifted her gaze to Luke. He rubbed his temples and went back to the laptop. She could see the strain on his face, the headache forming beneath his brow. He worked hard, too. Only he never gave himself a break. He never had any fun.

Maggie gazed out the window, at the perfectly beautiful winter day, at the snow Luke had predicted. "Let's get out of here," she said. "Let's ditch these files and go build a snowman." With a big, carrot nose, she thought, and a smile made of twigs.

He gave her an incredulous look. "I'm not going to waste valuable time goofing around. I've got a schedule to keep."

Not easily deterred, she moved away from the window and devised a brilliant plan. One way or another, she and Luke were going to play in the snow. "How about lunch? You have to eat, don't you?"

He shrugged. "I suppose."

"Then let's go out for lunch."

He agreed, albeit reluctantly, to take an hour off for a meal. Precisely one hour, he stipulated, sounding like the ex-military man that he was.

Maggie buttoned her coat and slipped on a pair of kidskin gloves. Luke reached for a leather jacket, then pulled a hand through his hair, smoothing a few stray locks into place.

Dressed for the weather, they exited the house, and he locked the door behind them. As he turned and strode toward his SUV, Maggie knelt to the ground. And then, as quickly as her hands would allow, she formed a snowball.

Rising, she took aim and heaved it. The snowball sailed through the air and hit Luke in the back, dissolving into a white burst as it made the connection.

He spun around, and Maggie swallowed her triumphant smile.

The first thing out of his mouth was a curse. The second was a complaint.

"Damn it. I dropped the keys." He kicked the fresh powder. "And now I've got to dig through this mess to find them."

She offered to help, thinking he had to be the biggest grump on earth. The snow wasn't that deep. How far could the keys have gone?

Luke put on his gloves, and they sifted through the powder, neither uttering a single word. Disgusted, Maggie turned her back and searched in another spot.

And that was when a huge clump of snow fell right on top of her head.

Stunned, she wiped away the moisture dripping onto her face. The sound of keys jangling caught her attention. She turned and saw Luke standing above her, a dastardly grin on his handsome face.

"You've been had," he said, shoving the keys back into his pocket, where they had apparently been all along.

"Oh, yeah?" Maggie wanted to hug him breathless, but instead she packed another snowball, making her intentions clear.

Instantly he ducked for cover, choosing a battle station on the other side of the car.

The war was on.

Three

Maggie peered around the tailgate, but saw neither hide nor hair of Luke. Her hide and her hair, on the other hand, were drenched. He'd outsmarted every maneuver she'd tried so far.

Where was he? Under the vehicle? Wedged against a tire? She had an arsenal of snowballs ready to go, just waiting for him to show his sneaky face.

Determined to win, she opted for another tactic. The damsel-in-distress ploy ought to work. A macho guy like Luke should fall for that. Her brothers usually did. Men, she thought with a feminine gleam in her eye, were natural-born suckers.

"It's time to quit," she called out. "I'm freezing, and I want to go inside."

She continued to peer around the SUV, armed with a carefully packed snowball. Testing the weight in her hand, she smiled. It was, in her estimation, a solid sphere of ice.

"Luke!" she called out again. "This isn't funny. I'm exhausted, and you have the keys to the house."

"Nice try, princess," a deep voice said from behind her.

She turned and saw Luke aiming a bucket of snow at her. Still clutching her ammunition, Maggie let out a girlish squeal and took off running.

Bucket in hand, he chased her.

They danced around a tree, back and forth, like foolhardy kids. There was no time to think, to stop and admire the husky sound of his laughter or the way his dark eyes crinkled when he smiled.

She was having too much fun to analyze the moment. And so was he.

Maggie tossed the snowball at him. It sailed past his shoulder and splattered against the tree. White flecks glistened against the bark, the edges icy and sharp.

Luke moved toward her, slowly, teasing her with the bucket, giving her a chance to turn tail and run.

Instead, she did something to catch him off guard. She charged him, full force, intending to knock the ammunition out of his hand.

The bucket went flying, and so did she.

When she tackled Luke, he lost his footing and took her down with him. Arms and legs tangling, they rolled, like snowmen toppling to the ground. Maggie's breath rushed out in gasping pants.

He ended up on top, his weight sinking into hers, powdery flakes fluttering around them. He wiped the snow from her face, his gloved hand brushing gently.

"Are you all right?" he asked.

"Yes." She touched his face, too. Then ran her hands through his hair, combing the dampness away from his forehead.

Their eyes met and held. Without speaking, they stared at each other, their emotions frozen in time.

It could have been a dream, she thought. A fantasy drifting on the edge of reality. If she looked past him, she would see a rainbow, an arc of gems shooting across the December sky.

He whispered her name, and the jewels grew brighter— diamonds, rubies, emeralds falling from the heavens.

Maggie and Luke moved at the same time, in the same instant. She drew him closer, and he lowered his head.

The wind whipped over them, and they kissed.

Desperately.

He sucked on her bottom lip, caught it with his teeth. The imaginary rainbow blurred her vision, sending sparks over every inch of her skin.

Thrusting his tongue into her mouth, he clasped both of her hands in his, taking possession, staking his claim.

Maggie wanted to possess him, too. To make Lucas Starwind hers. To take everything that he was and wrap him tightly around her heart. He tasted like heat and snow, like ice dripping over a long, dark, dangerous candle, the wick igniting into a flame.

A gust of cold air sliced over them, but neither noticed.

They kissed, again and again, questing for more—nibbling, licking, absorbing every thrilling sensation.

Luke released her hands, and they went after each other. She unzipped his jacket; he unbuttoned her coat. He slid his hips between her legs; she bumped his fly.

They were making love in their minds, mimicking the rocking, rubbing motion with their bodies. Maggie clung to the man in her arms. This was, she thought, the most wildly erotic moment of her life.

Until a neighbor's car door slammed.

Luke shot up like an arrow. Then he cursed, clearly chastising himself for losing control.

"You're going to catch pneumonia," he said, fumbling to rebutton her coat.

Maggie didn't think that was possible. She was as warm as sealing wax. And she wanted to melt all over him. But she knew the opportunity had passed.

Luke was Luke again. Tough. Tense. Guarded.

"Come on." He reached for her hand and drew her to her feet. "You need a hot bath. And something to eat."

She needed to kiss him again, she thought, but she didn't argue. She rather liked being protected by the big, tough detective. He actually swept her into his arms and carried her to the front door.

Luke Starwind was dark and dangerous. Exciting. When she'd slid her hands over those sturdy muscles, she'd felt the holstered gun he kept clipped to the back of his belt. It seemed, somehow, like an extension of his body, like part of the man he was. The Cherokee warrior, she thought. The former Green Beret.

He fumbled with his keys. Maggie put her head on his shoulder as he stepped over the threshold. Feeling delightfully feminine, she pressed her lips to his neck and smiled when he sucked in a tight breath.

He deposited her in the master bathroom, where a sunken tub awaited—an enormous, dark-green enclosure surrounded by rugged antiques. She caught a glimpse of his four-poster bed and tried not to swoon. His house was growing on her.

Feeling as boneless as a rag doll, she allowed him to remove her coat.

"Will you start a fire?" she asked, wishing he would undress her completely.

He didn't, of course. Her coat was as far as he went.

"Yeah. I'll heat up a can of soup, too."

"Thank you." She pressed a delicate kiss to his cheek and felt him shiver. "You're cold, too," she remarked.

"I'll dry off in the other bathroom."

He backed away and thrust a towel at her. Maggie accepted the offer, thinking how incredible using his soap was going to be.

She eyed a bulk of terry cloth hanging behind the door. "Can I wear your robe, Luke?"

"What?" He followed her gaze, a frown furrowing his brow. "No," he responded, his voice strained. "I'll get you a pair of sweats."

"All right." She shrugged as if his robe held little consequence. When he was gone, she decided, she would slip it on. Just for a second. Just to feel it caress her bare skin.

Luke washed his face, towel-dried his hair and slipped on a T-shirt and a pair of old, comfortable jeans. Next he built a fire and headed to the kitchen to heat some soup. He tried not to think about Maggie soaking in his tub, sleek and naked, her skin warm and flushed.

He'd behaved like a kid, goofing around in the snow, letting Maggie pull him under her playful spell. But worse yet, he'd lost complete control, kissing her until his body ached with a hot, feverish lust.

Dumping the soup into a pot, he added the required amount of water and reminded himself that Maggie was off-limits. Way off-limits. The last thing he needed was to get involved with a woman practically young enough to be his daughter. Luke rarely took a lover, and when he did, he made damn sure his partner was mature enough to handle a sex-only relationship.

Then again, he doubted free-spirited, frolic-in-the-snow Maggie was looking for a lifelong commitment. He'd seen

pictures of her in the society pages with her former beau—
a twenty-something Italian race-car driver. A live-for-the-
minute European playboy.

Which made Luke wonder what Maggie saw in a crusty,
pushing-forty P.I. like himself.

"Luke?"

Squaring his shoulders, he turned to acknowledge her.
She stood in the doorway, her freshly washed hair combed
away from her face, her blue-green eyes sparkling.

Luke squinted through a frown. What spell was she about
to cast? And how could a woman look downright breathtaking in a pair of standard-gray sweats?

His sweats, he reminded himself.

"That smells good," she said.

"It's ready." He reached for a cup. "Do you want crackers?"

When she nodded, he pulled a box from the cupboard.

Minutes later, they sat in front of the fire, sipping tomato
soup. Flames danced in the stone hearth, warming the room
with a flickering gold light. Maggie spooned up soggy
crackers and watched him through her magical eyes.

"Tell me what you said, Luke."

Confused, he shook his head. "What are you talking
about?"

"When we danced at Rafe's wedding reception. You said
something to me. Something in Cherokee."

He fought to steady his pulse. *A qua da nv do. My heart.*
He would never forget those words or the moment he'd said
them. "I don't recall saying anything."

She scooted closer. They sat cross-legged on a wool rug,
just a few feet apart. Her hair had begun to dry, and the fire
bathed her in an amber glow. She looked young and soft,
her skin scrubbed free of cosmetics.

"But you have to remember. They sounded so pretty."

She struggled to repeat the phrase. "I can hear them in my head, but I can't pronounce them."

He could hear them in his head, too. Could feel them pounding in his chest. "I'm sorry. I just don't remember."

Maggie glanced down at her soup, and Luke frowned. He knew his lie had hurt her feelings.

But how could he tell her that for an instant in time she had actually become part of his heart? He didn't understand why he'd felt such a tender, almost haunting connection to her. And he never wanted to go through something like that again. She had no right to touch his heart, not even for an instant.

"I bought a book about the Cherokee," she said. "I curled up one night in bed and read about your ancestors. It's a fascinating culture. So beautiful. So noble."

He placed his empty cup on the mantel. "I'm only half Cherokee." And he was neither noble nor beautiful.

Maggie watched him, and he felt self-conscious under her scrutiny. He knew she was studying his features—eyes lined with well-earned crow's-feet, a nose that had been broken on the worst day of his life, a jaw as hard as granite.

"It's still part of your legacy, Luke."

"So you bought that book because of me?"

"Yes." She tilted her head, her hair falling to one side. "The chapters about the Trail of Tears made me cry. All those people being forced to leave their homeland, starving and freezing and dying on the way."

Something inside him nearly shattered. In some small way, she had cried for him. "I'm Eastern Band Cherokee. My ancestors hid in the Great Smoky Mountains in order to escape removal." Men, women and children, he thought, whom the army had pledged to hunt down like wild dogs. But he supposed Maggie had read about that, too.

"Where do your parents live?" she asked, her voice still filled with emotion.

"My dad's dead."

"Oh. I'm sorry." She glanced at the fire. For a moment, they both fell silent.

He knew she was going to ask him about his mom next. Somehow, that hurt even more. His mother's sheltered, fragile lifestyle was a constant reminder of the pain his family had endured.

"Is your mom close by?"

"No. She lives in the country." In the same house where he grew up. The same quiet little farmhouse where the kidnapping had taken place.

"What does she look like?"

Like a woman who'd lost everything that mattered, he thought. "She's fair-skinned, and her hair is sort of a silvery-gray. It used to be brown."

Maggie smiled. "I bet she's pretty."

He swallowed the lump in his throat. "My dad thought so."

She finished her soup, placing the empty cup beside his. Uncrossing her legs, she drew her knees up. Her face was a wash of golden hues from the fire, her eyes a watery shade of blue. He wondered how many times a day they changed color.

"Do you have any brothers and sisters?"

The question hit him like a fist. He clenched his stomach muscles to sustain the impact. "No," he said as his heart went numb.

Not anymore.

The next day Maggie awakened to the sound of a screeching telephone. She pushed through the mosquito netting that draped her brass bed and squinted at the clock.

Groaning, she nearly knocked the phone off the dresser. Who called at five o'clock on a Sunday morning? On her private line, no less?

"This better be important," she said into the receiver.

"It's Luke."

A shiver shot straight up her spine. She'd worn Luke's sweats home yesterday. And needing to feel connected to him throughout the night, she'd also slept in them. The fleece-lined fabric brushed her skin like warm, masculine hands.

His hands, she thought as she heard him breathe into the phone.

"What's going on?" she asked, trying to sound professional. Clearly an early-morning call from Luke related to business. As far as she knew, he didn't make personal calls, at least not to her. "Did you get a breakthrough in the case?"

"No. But I picked up your bodyguard at the airport, and we're on our way over. So get out of bed and put on some coffee. He's moving into your place today."

Maggie shot up like a rocket, nearly tearing the mosquito net from the ceiling. Her bodyguard? "You're not going to sic some big, burly brute on me." In spite of her family's wealth and celebrity, she did her damnedest to live a normal life. Which meant no maids, chauffeurs, cooks or bodyguards. She cleaned her own house, drove her own car and fixed her own meals. Granted, her house was a two-million-dollar loft, her car was a Lamborghini and she purchased her food from a gourmet market, but she was still self-sufficient.

"I have the most sophisticated alarm system ever devised," she went on. "I don't need a bodyguard."

"Too bad. Your brother already agreed with me that Bruno should move in with you until this case is solved."

Her brother. She should have known Rafe had a hand in this. He and Luke seemed to think she was some sort of helpless female. "What kind of stupid name is Bruno?" She pictured a no-neck, muscle-bound Gestapo guarding her front door.

"I've seen Bruno in action, Maggie. And I'm not changing my mind about hiring him. We'll see you in fifteen minutes. And if you don't let us in, we'll break in, proving to you how useless that alarm system of yours is. You don't even have a security camera."

She fumed. She raged. She paced the floor with darts in her eyes. Luke was going to suffer for this. And so was Bruno. She would make the bodyguard's assignment a living hell, ditching him every chance she got.

Maggie washed her face and brushed her teeth, but she didn't change her clothes or put on a pot of coffee. If Luke wanted freshly brewed coffee, she would gladly kick his rear all the way to Colombia, where he could pick his own damn beans.

Luke and Bruno arrived in the estimated fifteen minutes. Luke buzzed her, and she pressed the remote and opened the security gate at the entrance of an underground parking structure, then shot out of the loft and waited at the indoor elevator that led to her living quarters. The industrial building had been remodeled to suit her needs, but she'd kept the old-fashioned, gated elevator because she liked its vintage style.

She heard the elevator ascending, and when it stopped, her jaw went slack.

Luke's companion was on a leash.

Bruno, it appeared, was a dog. The most powerful-looking creature she'd ever seen.

"That's my bodyguard?"

Luke and the beast exited the elevator. "He's not what you expected?"

"You know damn well I thought Bruno was a man."

The dog didn't react to his name or to the sharp tone in Maggie's voice. Luke, however, had the gall to arch an eyebrow at her. Apparently he didn't care that he'd ruffled her feathers at five in the morning.

"Now why would I hire another man to move in with you? Hell, Maggie, I could have done that myself."

Then why didn't you? she wanted to ask. Why didn't you become my personal bodyguard? My roommate?

Because he'd given the job to Bruno.

She shifted her attention to the dog. He stood about thirty inches tall and probably weighed a good two hundred pounds. Heavy-boned, with a fawn-colored body, his muzzle bore a dark mask.

"What is he?" she asked.

"An English mastiff."

She studied Bruno's serious face. She doubted the big dog would ever roll over with his paws in the air, begging for a belly rub. Maggie patted his head, deciding she would have to loosen him up. Teach him to do dumb doggie things. The poor fellow behaved like an armed guard with a rifle up his butt.

"There's no point in standing in the hall," she said, inviting Luke and Bruno into her home.

The first thing Luke noticed about Maggie's loft was the skylight. Dawn blazed from the ceiling, sending lavender streaks throughout the room.

Her decor was bold, yet decidedly female. A variety of textures, ranging from watered silk to carved-and-painted woods, made up the living room. Leafy plants grew from clay pots and scented candles dripped melted wax. The oak floors were whitewashed, and one entire wall was covered with a mural of mermaids rising from the sea.

Instinctively, he knew Maggie had painted it. He felt the enchantment flow over him like a cool, sensual wine.

Moonlight and mermaids. He turned to look at her, and saw that she watched Bruno instead.

Luke let out the breath he'd been holding, shrugging off the sexual pull.

"Is Bruno one of those German-trained dogs?" she asked. "The ones that compete in international trials?"

"You mean Schutzhund? No, he's not." Luke had decided a Schutzhund-titled dog wasn't what Maggie needed. "Bruno is familiar with the perils of everyday life."

Maggie met his gaze. He moved away from the mermaids and focused on familiarizing her with the dog. "I'll teach you his verbal commands. He'll respond to you without a problem." A business associate of Luke's supplied dogs to police and military canine units, as well as private citizens. "Bruno has been trained to protect women. He's stopped kidnappers and stalkers right in their tracks. He'll keep you safe."

She regarded the mastiff with a curious expression. "Does he fetch?"

For a moment Luke could only stare. He'd provided her with one of the most expensive, sought-after protection dogs in the world, an animal that adapted to a new environment without the slightest hesitation, and she wanted to know if he retrieved tennis balls?

"Bruno is a bodyguard, Maggie."

She ran a manicured hand through her night-tousled hair. Luke had no idea why she was still wearing his sweats, but he thought she looked as wildly erotic as one of the naked mermaids.

"Can he shake? Or high-five?"

"He's a personal protection dog," Luke reiterated, clenching his jaw.

"I'm well aware of that. But I don't see anything wrong with teaching him to do a few doggie tricks. He deserves to have a little fun."

Luke caught Maggie's gaze and saw a spark of mischief brewing in those muse-magic eyes. "Don't you dare ruin this animal." He envisioned her encouraging a two-hundred-pound, muscle-bound mastiff to sit up and beg for table scraps. "I don't want you distracting him from his job."

"I hope he knows how to kiss. All dogs should kiss."

Good Lord. Luke glanced at Bruno. The canine sat, watching his new mistress. The dog had been taught *not* to lick people's faces, which made perfect sense to Luke. "I'm pretty sure he drools. Will that do?"

She smiled like a siren. "It's a start."

Maggie brewed a pot of coffee, and they spent the next three hours going over Bruno's commands. Luke offered to come by every night after work to help her exercise the big dog.

Maggie seemed pleased, and he warned himself not to get too attached. No hugs, no kisses, no foreplay in the snow.

"Are you and Bruno ready for the grand tour?" she asked.

"Sure."

The loft was six thousand square feet of artistic inspiration. Bruno had plenty of corners and shadowy areas to explore.

They went from room to room, and Luke found Maggie's home strangely alluring, particularly her bedroom.

A mosquito net draped her unmade bed. He pictured her sleeping there, her hair fanned across satin pillows. The color scheme was warm and inviting, the textures rich and smooth.

Bruno sniffed, taking in every scent. Luke could smell a heady blend of candles, incense and French perfume.

In that intoxicating instant he wanted to break his self-imposed rule and kiss her. Pull her onto the bed and run his hands all over that long, luscious body.

"Come on," she said. "I want you to see my work."

He drew a rough breath and followed Maggie to her studio.

The walls, he noticed, were splattered with paint, as if she'd attacked them in an emotional rage. Art supplies littered the floor. Canvases were stacked everywhere. Floor-to-ceiling windows illuminated the enormous room.

Her work reflected her moods. A life-size watercolor of a wood nymph was blatantly sexual, whereas the portrait of a baby dragon projected sheer whimsy. Each piece was inspired from fantasy or folklore, portraying mythical creatures.

He wondered if she'd ever painted a muse. He decided not to ask.

"This is my latest series," she said, displaying three canvases for him to view.

He studied the paintings, analyzing each one before he moved on to the next. The first one depicted a wide-eyed little boy peering at a leprechaun. The second was a fair-haired toddler with a fairy on her shoulder.

And the third painting had Luke nearly dropping to his knees.

His breath shot out, and he curled his fingers to keep from touching the beautiful, haunting, heartbreaking image.

"She could be my sister," he whispered. The profile of a young girl filled the canvas, jet-black hair blowing around her face, a tiny winged horse fluttering from her outstretched hands.

He turned to look at Maggie, who watched him through silent eyes. "How did you know?" he asked, his voice breaking. "How did you know that we buried her with her favorite toy?"

A tiny winged horse.

Four

"**Y**our sister?" Maggie placed her hand on his shoulder. "Oh, God, Luke. I didn't know you had a sister. Or that she died."

Then she couldn't have known about the winged horse, he thought. Her painting was simply a coincidence or an omen or a connection that had no logical explanation.

Luke drew a breath. "Can we go outside? I need some air."

"Of course."

They took the elevator to the roof where Maggie had created a patio. A barbecue pit was formed of stone, with chairs gathered around it. Snow melted on the ground, and the wind blew mildly.

Luke stood near the rail and scanned the sweeping lake-front view. He could see the Art Institute and the glass-and-steel structure of the Connelly Tower. He assumed Maggie enjoyed the city traffic and the sound of the el train.

He turned to look at her. Bruno remained by her side, already protecting her. That gave Luke a measure of relief.

"Will you tell me about your sister?" she asked.

He knew he couldn't hide the truth. Not now. Not after his reaction to Maggie's painting. "Her name was Gwen. I used to call her Lady Guinevere." He gazed at the fire pit, his heart clenching with the memory. "She loved legends and fables and pretty fairy tales."

"What happened to her, Luke?"

"She was murdered," he responded. "And it was my fault."

Maggie reached for a chair, her breath catching. "You can't mean that."

"When my father was dying, he asked me to protect her." To be the man of the house, he recalled. The young warrior. "But I didn't keep her safe. I let a stranger come into our home. He kidnapped Gwen, and then he killed her."

Maggie's face paled, and Luke sat across from her, preparing to tell her everything, every detail that made him ache.

"I was twelve and Gwen was eight. Our father had died three months before, and Mom was visiting a friend in the neighborhood. She had been grieving very deeply, and this was the first time she'd socialized since his death."

As Luke spoke, his mind drifted back in time, back to the day that had destroyed what was left of his family.

Gwen, dressed in pink shorts and a white top, had played on the porch. She'd made a castle out of a cardboard box for the king and queen she'd cut out from a coloring book. The winged horse sat next to her, waiting to soar across the sky. The air was warm, the sun setting behind the hills in a reddish-gold hue.

Luke watched his sister from the screen door, then went

into the kitchen to toss a couple of TV dinners in the oven. He chose fried chicken for Gwen and meat loaf for himself. The mashed potatoes always tasted fake, but his mother wouldn't be back in time to cook what he considered real food.

But that didn't matter, he thought, because he was glad she'd gone out. She still cried a lot, and he never knew what to say to make her feel better. Luke missed his dad, too.

Ten minutes later, he heard Gwen talking to someone on the porch. Luke went to the door and saw a fair-haired man crouching next to his sister.

"His car broke down in front of our house," she said as the man raised to his full height. "I told him nobody was home but you and me."

The quiet stranger was tall, with narrow shoulders, skinny arms and lean hips. His skin was pale, his eyebrows as blond as his hair. Luke thought the guy looked frailer than a man should.

Gwen got up and came toward the screen door. "Can he use our phone? He needs to call a tow truck."

"Sure." Luke figured the guy didn't know how to fix his own car. He didn't seem like the mechanic type. Plus, it was obvious he'd gotten lost and was too embarrassed to admit it. Their old farmhouse was on a dirt road, miles from the main highway.

"I really appreciate this," the man said.

"No problem." They went inside, and Luke showed him to the den. He pointed to the phone, which sat on a cluttered rolltop desk. The Yellow Pages were next to it. "Try Harvey's Garage. I'm pretty sure they have a tow truck."

"Thank you. I will."

Luke turned away to see what Gwen was doing. She'd gone into the kitchen, and he figured she was going to bug him about dinner, which would seem rude in front of the stranger.

Within seconds, a burst of pain exploded in the back of Luke's head. He knew instantly the man had hit him with a heavy object, possibly even a gun. He tried to call Gwen's name, to tell her to run, but the stranger hit him again. And this time, the force knocked him down.

His face crashed against the corner of a table. And then he felt the sickening warmth of blood running from his nose and into his mouth.

His sister dashed into the room. He saw her feet, then heard her panicked scream—just once before the world went black.

For a moment, Maggie and Luke remained silent, the wind stirring around them.

His eyes were dark and filled with pain. She longed to touch him, to bring him close to her heart.

He met her gaze, and she thought about how much he was hurting. She couldn't imagine the horror of losing a sibling. Maggie had grown up with a houseful of brothers and sisters, and she adored them all. "I'm sorry," she said.

"Two days later, a farmer found Gwen's body in an empty field. The weeds were so high, he nearly tripped over her." Luke's voice broke. "The lot was for sale, and he was looking for a place to buy. But he found my sister instead."

Maggie's eyes filled with tears. She pictured the little girl she had painted, dumped in a field of weeds. She had no explanation why her painting resembled Luke's sister. The dark-haired child and the tiny winged horse had stemmed from her imagination.

"The things that bastard did to her. And I trusted him. I let him into our home."

"You couldn't have known he was dangerous. Or that he preyed on children."

Luke released an audible breath. "The police caught him, but that didn't bring closure. Not to me. When I testified at his trial, I sat there envisioning what he did to Gwen and thinking how much I wanted to kill him."

"Is he still in prison?"

"Yes. He was up for parole in September. I attended the hearing. I wanted to make damn sure that bastard wasn't paroled. There's no such thing as a rehabilitated pedophile." He gazed out at the city. "But no matter what I do to make things right, I still feel like I have blood on my hands."

"What happened to Gwen wasn't your fault, Luke."

"Yes, it was. And so was Tom Reynolds's murder."

"Your partner?" Maggie tried to comprehend his logic. "You were out of town when Tom was killed."

"That's exactly my point. I was at the parole hearing while my partner was being ambushed. If I had been here, I could have given Tom the backup he needed."

So much unwarranted guilt, she thought. So much pain. Lucas Starwind wanted to save the world all by himself. "You're one man. There's only so much you can do."

"There's no way you can understand how I feel. You haven't lived my life."

But she wanted to. She wanted to live inside him, to be part of him. She looked into his eyes and saw the emptiness she wished she could fill.

Placing her hands on her lap, she felt them tremble. Heaven help her. She knew what was happening.

Maggie was falling desperately in love, losing her heart to a reclusive, tortured man.

"Are you cold?" he asked.

She blinked. "What?"

"You're shivering."

Because I'm in love, she thought. And afraid I won't be able to keep you. Their paths had crossed, but Luke seemed determined to remain alone, to punish himself for tragedies that were beyond his control.

Maggie glanced at the melting snow, at the slush around her feet. How could she help him? How could she bandage wounds that refused to heal?

"Come on," he said. "We'll go inside and warm up."

Once they were back in the loft, Luke poured two cups of coffee. He doctored hers with sugar and cream, and she found the strength to smile. Already he knew she liked her coffee light and sweet.

Bruno remained by Maggie's side. She pictured all of them—man, woman and dog—living together, happy and content.

Luke frowned, and she realized how hopeful her fantasy was. Luke was investigating her family's case, and Bruno was her temporary bodyguard. They weren't exactly a family.

"I can't stay too much longer," he said.

"It's Sunday. Don't tell me you're working today."

"No."

"Then what are you going to do?" she asked, wishing he wasn't so evasive. He'd told her about his sister, but she knew her painting had stunned him into revealing that part of his life.

He sipped his coffee. "There's just someplace I have to be."

"Where?" she pressed.

"Nothing that concerns you."

Maggie sighed. Luke's dismissal hurt. Everything he did concerned her. He was the man she loved, the dark-eyed warrior who had stolen his way into her dreams. And Maggie believed in pursuing dreams. "Why won't you tell me?"

"Because it's personal."

How personal? she wondered, suddenly suspicious. Was he seeing another woman?

Of course he was. What other explanation could there be? Men weren't always the most honest creatures. Even her father had stepped out on her mother. Although it had happened over thirty years ago, and her parents had been separated at the time, the mighty Grant Connelly had still cheated. Maggie's half brother Seth was proof of the affair.

"I can't believe you're doing this to me."

Leaning against the counter, Luke continued to sip his drink. "Doing what?"

"Cheating," she snapped. "Dating someone else."

He arched an eyebrow. "Since when have you and I been an item?"

She narrowed her eyes, deciding she would tear his lover's hair out. Strand by strand. "You kissed me."

"That's not exactly a commitment."

Hurt and anger rose, brimming like a volcano. "Are you seeing someone or not?"

He almost smiled, telling her that he found her envy amusing. That ticked her off even more. Luke treated her like a crush-crazed teenager, like a girl who wrote his name all over her notebook, doodling hearts around it. True, she thrived on the lure of romance, but that didn't make her immature.

"Damn it. Give me a straight answer."

He cocked his head. "Your eyes change color. Did you know that? They're blue when you're sad or worried. And green when you're spewing that Irish temper of yours."

"Don't change the subject," she retorted, even though she was flattered that he'd looked that closely at her eyes.

His near smile turned to a frown. "Okay. You want the

truth. Here it is. I visit my mom on Sundays. I drive out to the country because she won't come to the city.''

So the ''other woman'' was his mother. Now Maggie felt foolish. But people in love were allowed to act foolish, weren't they? ''Doesn't she like the city?''

''She's agoraphobic.''

Maggie stepped forward. ''She's afraid of open spaces?''

''That's the literal explanation, but it's more complicated than that. She's afraid of going places that will cause her to panic, places away from home.''

''Why?'' was all she could think to ask.

''I'm not sure. But I think it's because she wasn't home when Gwen was kidnapped. So her way of feeling safe is to stay home, to be where she thinks she should have been that day.''

Maggie drew a breath. Did Luke blame himself for his mother's phobia? Did it make him feel even more responsible for his sister's death? There was so much hurt in his family, so many sad, empty hearts. ''Is she under a doctor's care?''

He shook his head. ''When it first happened, I didn't know that she was having anxiety attacks. All I knew was that Gwen was dead, and my mom didn't want to leave the house anymore. She didn't tell me that she was panicking in public situations.'' He set his empty cup in the sink. ''Once I learned what agoraphobia was, it was too late. She refused to discuss her condition with me.''

''Does she go out at all now?''

''A little bit, but never very far. She has a live-in housekeeper. Someone who shops and runs errands for her.''

Someone, Maggie suspected, Luke had hired.

He checked his watch. ''I better hit the road. It's a long drive.'' He reached down and patted the dog, then looked up at Maggie. ''Don't go anywhere without Bruno.''

"I won't." She walked Luke to the door. He turned, and they stared at each other, but only for a moment.

When he entered the elevator, she watched him depart, wishing she had the courage to tell him that she loved him.

Maggie headed for her studio, Bruno on her heels. She gazed around the room and locked onto the painting she'd yet to title—the watercolor of the little girl who looked like Gwen.

How did you know? Luke had asked her. How did you know that we buried her with her favorite toy?

Maggie studied the tiny horse fluttering from the child's outstretched hands. She remembered painting it, feeling each delicate wing come to life.

"Are you Gwen?" she asked the painting, tears filling her eyes. "Did you slip into my subconscious because you wanted me to fall in love with your brother? To touch his heart? To heal his soul?"

Maggie wanted that, too. But she didn't know how to reach Luke, how to prove that they belonged together.

Bruno cocked his big, fawn-colored head, and Maggie smiled through her tears. "I'll think of something," she said to the dog, the child and the tiny winged horse. "I'll find a way to make Luke mine."

On Monday morning, Maggie entered Rey-Star Investigations attired in an emerald-green suit and gold jewelry. Bruno, the dog she'd come to think of as a big, furry accessory, strode beside her. She'd bought him a jeweled collar that made him look less like a bodyguard and more like a pampered pet.

Carol glanced up from her computer and smiled. "Hello, Ms. Connelly. Oh, my, who's your handsome friend?"

Maggie introduced Bruno and explained that Luke had

gotten security clearance for the mastiff to accompany her to the office.

"May I pet him?"

"Of course."

Carol came around her desk to fuss over the dog.

Bruno gazed up at the buxom blonde and drooled.

When Maggie entered Luke's office, she was smiling. He, on the other hand, sat at his desk, wearing his usual scowl.

She removed her overcoat. "Good morning."

He lifted his gaze and looked her over, those dark eyes traveling from the top of her head to the tips of her Italian pumps. "You're late," he said.

"Bruno wanted to sleep in."

"Very funny." He glanced at the dog, then back at her. "In the future, I expect both of you to be on time. Now go to your own office and get to work."

She thought about the files on her desk, the drudge of paperwork. "I'm having a cup of tea first." After releasing Bruno from his leash, she walked over to the bar and pressed the red spigot, filling her cup with hot water. Digging through an assortment of teas Luke kept on hand for his clients, she chose chamomile, hoping it would soothe her nerves. She'd stayed up most of the night plotting her strategy. And this morning she intended to enforce a carefully developed plan.

She sweetened her tea, then took a seat and crossed her legs. Eyeing Luke over the rim of her cup, she studied him. He looked like what he was—a former Green Beret, mature, highly skilled, superbly trained. Not that she didn't admire his military background or the fact that it made him a more effective P.I., but it also made him a difficult civilian to deal with.

Luke was an expert at unconventional warfare. Which was why she had devised a challenge with which to bait him. All is fair in love and war, she thought, placing her cup on the edge of his glossy black desk.

"I'd like to make a deal with you," she said.

He released an impatient breath. "I suppose you want to come in at ten instead of nine every morning."

"This doesn't have anything to do with me working here."

"Then what's it about?" He checked his watch, telling her that she was wasting valuable time.

"I want the opportunity to heal that tortured soul of yours."

He looked up from his watch, his narrowed gaze latching onto hers. "What the hell are you up to? Is this a joke?"

"No." This is my heart, she thought. Everything I have to give. "Let's face it, Luke. You're a tense, troubled man. If you're not angry, you're sad."

He gave her a pointed look. "And you're going to turn me into Mr. Chipper?"

Maggie couldn't help but smile. "Not exactly."

He leaned back in his chair. Today he wore various shades of gray. The gunmetal tie and a charcoal jacket reminded her of a rainstorm. He would never be Mr. Chipper.

"I'm going to teach you to stop punishing yourself," she said. "To live life and have a little fun."

"As opposed to suffering with inner demons?"

"That's one way of putting it."

"I see. And what do I have to do in return? Sign my name in blood?"

"No." She reached for her tea and took a dainty sip, giving herself a moment to form the words. Suddenly her heart pounded so hard, she feared it would burst through her blouse. "I'm offering you a dare. A marriage dare," she added, emphasizing the challenge.

He came forward in his chair. "Excuse me?"

"You have to promise to marry me if I can make you stop hurting. If I can save you from your pain." He needed so desperately to live, she thought. To experience hope and joy and the beauty love had to offer.

Luke couldn't decide if she was on the level, so he assessed her body language, and when that didn't help, he went right for her eyes.

They were as green as her suit, which told him nothing. Rather than reveal her emotions, they reflected the color she wore. He wondered if she had camouflaged herself on purpose.

"A marriage dare?" he asked, struggling to comprehend her logic.

"Yes," she responded, giving nothing away.

Luke leaned his elbows on the desk. Maggie Connelly could have just about any man she wanted yet she'd zeroed in on him. Why? What made him so appealing?

The challenge, he realized. She thrived on challenge, and he was the biggest contest of all. The aloof detective, the confirmed bachelor. She considered him the unattainable prize.

"I accept," he said, deciding he'd beat her at her own game. "But I'm adding another clause. I'll promise to marry you if you can save me, but you have to do it before the stroke of midnight on New Year's Eve."

She gave him an incredulous look. "That's less than a month away."

"Take it or leave it, Cinderella. Those are the terms."

Maggie chewed her bottom lip and glanced at Bruno. The dog looked back at her. "I want it in writing, with Bruno as our witness."

She was turning to a dog for support? Clearly she was in over her head. "No problem. You type up the contract, and I'll sign it."

"Once you commit, you can't back out," she said.

"I won't need to," he told her.

She headed to her office to draw up the contract, and he returned to the file on his desk. Not even a muse named Maggie could save Lucas Starwind from his demons.

Five

Luke, Maggie and Elena Delgado Connelly gathered around the table in the conference room at Rey-Star Investigations, studying the reports Elena had given Luke months ago.

Elena was the Special Investigative Unit detective the Chicago P.D. had first assigned to the case, and although she was no longer on active duty, Luke had asked her to come in. He intended to check and recheck the facts, giving Maggie the benefit of discussing the case with Elena—the only cop who had been entrusted with the truth about the cancer virus.

The women, of course, already knew each other on a personal level. During the course of the investigation, Elena had become a member of the Connelly clan, falling in love with and marrying Maggie's twenty-seven-year-old brother, Brett.

Luke shifted uncomfortably in his chair. He didn't intend

for that to happen to him. In spite of the ''marriage dare,'' he wasn't going to marry Maggie Connelly. Nor was he going to fall in love. Or have babies, he thought, glancing at Elena's four-month-old daughter.

Madison Connelly sat on her mother's lap, chewing the corner of a manila envelope. Luke was doing his damnedest to ignore her, but she kept watching him, mimicking his every move.

He'd never felt so self-conscious in his life.

He ran his hand through his hair; she reached for the fancy headband in hers. He frowned; she made an odd little scowling face.

''I bought a book on child development,'' Maggie said, causing Luke to glance her way.

What was she up to now? he wondered. Trying to add a baby clause to the marriage dare?

''Within two months Madison might be crawling,'' she went on, smiling at her niece. ''Or giving it her best shot.''

''She already is,'' Elena proclaimed. She laughed and bounced the baby, who seemed enthralled with the conversation. ''Sometimes she actually manages to move backward.''

Like a diaper-clad caboose, Luke thought, chugging along in reverse.

''So how does it feel to be a full-time mommy?'' Maggie asked her sister-in-law.

''I don't know if I can describe it.'' Suddenly the other woman looked soft and dreamy with her tawny-brown hair and pastel-colored sweater. ''I loved my job, but Madison and Brett are my life. Family means everything.''

She rubbed her cheek against her daughter's head. The tender gesture made Luke's heart ache. He had vowed long ago not to have children. He couldn't face each day wondering and worrying if his kids were safe. Gwen's kidnapping had taught him a painful lesson he'd never forget.

As the child leaned into her mother, he noticed the syrupy expression on Maggie's face. Luke decided he'd had enough.

"Excuse me, ladies, but do you think we could get back to work?"

All three females narrowed their eyes at him. He assumed his tone of voice, rather than his actual words, had irked little Madison. He almost apologized, then chose to hold his ground.

This was a business meeting not a baby convention.

Elena recovered first. She opened a file and glanced at the contents inside. Handing it to Maggie, she said, "This is Rocky Palermo."

"The Kelly hit man?"

Elena nodded, and Luke leaned over Maggie's shoulder, grateful their meeting was back on track. The man in the picture was broad-faced, his black hair scalped in a military-style cut. The scar that ran down the side of his neck protruded like a pale vein.

"Take a good look," Luke told her. "He could show up anytime, anywhere. Rocky is the Kellys' prime enforcer." He saw her shudder, so he touched her hand, running his fingers over her knuckles. "He's responsible for killing King Thomas and Prince Marc."

"Even in disguise, Rocky could be recognizable," Elena added. "He's willing to change his appearance, but not to the degree of altering his physique. He's proud of those muscles and likes to show them off."

"That figures. A conceited hit man." Maggie lifted the picture and held it next to her face. When she lowered it, baby Madison squealed.

That started a game of peekaboo with Maggie at the helm

and Elena beaming with maternal pride. Luke found himself in the middle, not knowing what to do. The baby shifted her gaze to him, searching, he assumed, for his approval.

She was a pretty little thing, a munchkin with a cap of black hair and expressive blue eyes. She wore a girlish ensemble of lace, denim and bows. Tiny white shoes, polished to a perfect shine, encased her feet. Frilly socks flared at her ankles.

Somehow, she made Rocky Palermo seem insignificant. She'd reduced the hit man's picture to a goofy, hand-clapping game.

Luke decided she deserved the attention she was getting. He flashed her a masculine smile. She rewarded him with a toothless grin.

And at that moment, at that surprisingly tender moment, he wondered how it would feel to be a father.

But as an image of Gwen's bruised and battered body came to mind, he drew a rough, gut-clenching breath.

Turning away, Luke glanced out the window. A gray haze covered the sky, floating across the city like a dark cloud.

There was no point in fooling himself. He could never handle being a parent.

Maggie opened the door, and Luke entered her loft. She'd given him the security code to the parking structure and a key to her home, but he hadn't been inclined to use either.

He frowned at her, an expression she'd come to know well.

"You're not ready," he said, stating the obvious.

Maggie stood before him in a silk robe. She'd done her hair and makeup, but she hadn't chosen her wardrobe yet. "I just have to get dressed." And she was nervous about their outing. Today she was meeting Luke's mother.

She glanced at her half-eaten breakfast on the dining-room table. Without thinking, she picked up her plate and set it on the floor.

Bruno gobbled up the remains, and Luke's jaw nearly dropped.

"You've been feeding that dog table scraps? Damn it, Maggie, I told you not to give him any junk. I promised his trainer you'd keep him on a strict diet."

Maggie knew the dog would be returned to his trainer once this case was over, but she couldn't resist spoiling him. "Eggs aren't junk. They're protein."

Luke eyed Bruno critically. "He looks like he's put on a few pounds. That's not good, you know. Mastiffs tend to get obese." The detective studied the dog from another angle. "You're not giving him snacks, are you?"

"No," she lied. She'd taught Bruno to shake. He was a fast learner with a fondness for corn chips and jelly beans.

"Are you sure?"

"Yes." She picked up the plate. The dog had lapped it clean. Still feeling anxious, she headed to the kitchen and poured Luke a cup of coffee, hoping that would placate him.

He accepted the offer and told her to hurry up and get dressed.

Maggie turned away, then spun back around. "Why did you invite me to go with you this morning?" He'd called at seven, asking if she wanted to meet his mother. The unexpected invitation had nearly stunned her speechless.

"It was my mom's idea."

"Really? She wants to meet me?"

"Why wouldn't she? You're famous."

Maggie's hope deflated. Mrs. Starwind was expecting a celebrity, someone she'd read about in the gossip columns. "You didn't tell her about our agreement, did you?"

"Our agreement? You mean that crazy marriage dare? Of course not. Now put on some clothes so we can get going."

Getting dressed wasn't a simple task. Maggie paced her room, hurt by Luke's indifference. He wasn't taking her seriously. True, daring him to marry her had been a bold proposition, but in the process, she'd offered to heal his heart. Couldn't he see what that really meant? Wasn't it obvious that she cared about him? Short of admitting out-right that she'd fallen in love, the marriage dare was the best she could do.

She reached for a sweater, then discarded it onto the bed. Seven outfits later, she still couldn't decide what to wear. Luke's mother wanted to meet the glamorous Maggie Con-nelly, yet Maggie wanted to present a genuine image, not the heiress the media had created. Then again, if she showed up looking too casual, Mrs. Starwind might be disappointed.

A knock sounded. She opened the door a crack.

Luke peered at her through the narrow space. "Are you okay? It's taking you forever."

She glanced at the clock. Thirty-five minutes had passed. "I'm accessorizing."

He rolled his eyes. "This isn't a fashion show. Just throw on some jeans."

Easy for him to say, she thought. He was ruggedly hand-some without the least bit of effort. Scuffed boots and faded Levi's added to his appeal.

Bruno appeared at Luke's feet. Sniffing curiously, he nudged his way into the room, pushing the door wider.

Maggie shot a quick glance over her shoulder and winced. Her bed was filled with designer rejects.

But when she turned back, she saw that Luke wasn't pay-ing attention to her fashion fiasco. His gaze was fixed on her body.

Her robe had come undone, exposing her bra and panties.

Maggie froze, struggling to catch her breath. Suddenly the air turned hot and muggy. Silk clung to her skin like steam from a torrid summer rain. Beneath the skimpy bra, her breasts tingled, her nipples rising to taut peaks.

She wanted to kiss Luke, to draw his mouth to hers and devour him. But instead she let him look, hoping he would touch.

He did.

He lifted his hand and rubbed his fingers over her lips. She licked his thumb and watched him shudder.

And then they stared at each other. A stretch of silence ensued, but their gazes never faltered.

Finally he moved his hand to her neck, and then to her robe. When he brought his other hand forward and closed the silk garment, his fingers brushed her nipples.

Deliberately. Accidentally. She wasn't sure.

"Get dressed," he whispered before he turned and walked away.

Maggie leaned against the door, her knees nearly buckling. How was she supposed to emerge from her room acting as if nothing had happened?

For the next fifteen minutes Luke sat on the sofa staring at the mermaid mural. Because he was tempted to touch the painting, to run his hands over each sensual siren, he tried to think of something casual to say when Maggie came out of her room. Something to douse his desire, something to ease the tension.

But he couldn't focus on anything except the heat running through his veins.

"Are they calling to you?"

"What?" Luke's heart bumped his chest. He turned away from the mural and saw Maggie. He hadn't heard her approach, yet she was there, like an apparition.

"The mermaids. Are they calling to you?"

"Yes," he answered honestly. And so was Maggie. Suddenly his mind was filled with an image of making love to her in the ocean, moonlit water lapping their skin. He could almost feel the warmth, the wetness, the motion of sliding between her legs.

"They called to me, too," she said, lowering herself to the sofa. "One night when I couldn't sleep, I read about mermaid sightings in the nineteenth century. And at dawn I started that mural."

"Who sighted them?" he asked, wondering if she believed the sea creatures were real.

"There are documented accounts from schoolmasters and explorers, but mostly they came from fishermen. In some cases, the mermaids had been caught in herring nets or tangled in fishing wire."

Luke glanced at the mural, then back at Maggie. "Did the fishermen set them free?"

She nodded. "In one instance, on the Isle of Man, they kept a mermaid for three days, but she wouldn't eat or drink, so they released her back into the ocean. They said she was very beautiful, perfectly formed. Above the waist, she resembled a young woman, and below she was a fish, with fins and a huge spreading tale."

"What about mermen?"

"There have been sightings of them, too." She met his gaze, her eyes a clear shade of aqua. "Someday I'm going to paint lovers from the sea. A merman, with a mermaid in his arms."

Luke had to catch his breath. "How will they make love?"

She smoothed her hair, combing her fingers through the golden highlights. She looked long and lean, dressed in jeans and an embroidered blouse that seemed as delicate as dandelions.

''They'll become human. And they'll join the way people do.''

''Why will they become human?'' he asked, mesmerized by her imagination.

''Because they've been touched by magic.''

Luke moistened his lips. ''How often will this spell occur?''

''Once a year, but only for an hour. So every time it happens, they'll be frantic for each other.''

He pictured them, the enchanted lovers from the sea, tangled in each other's arms, caressing and kissing, their damp bodies feverish with lust. They would make love in the water and then on the shore, stars shimmering in the sky and sand glistening on their skin.

It was, Luke realized, the same fantasy he'd had about Maggie.

He met her gaze and saw his own hunger shining back at him.

They didn't speak, but there didn't seem to be anything to say. Their eyes said it all. They both wanted the same thing.

This was madness, he thought. No matter how seductive, how incredibly erotic Maggie was to him, she wasn't the appropriate lover for a man his age.

''I was seventeen when you were born,'' he said, suddenly thinking out loud.

She blinked. ''What?''

''Nothing. Never mind.'' He stood, forcing himself to gain his composure. ''We better go.''

She came to her feet, then tilted her head. ''I'm an adult, Luke.''

Barely, he thought. She'd taken her first legal drink just the year before, and he'd downed his first legal beer in what seemed like a lifetime ago.

He grabbed his jacket, and Maggie reached for her purse, a tan shoulder bag that matched a pair of snakeskin boots. She'd accessorized all right, right down to the diamond studs winking in her ears and the gold bracelets shining on her wrists. Her jacket was vintage leather, a fringed number from the late sixties. The decade before she'd been born, Luke reminded himself. She had no recollection of hippies, Vietnam or men walking on the moon.

Luke might have been a kid then, but he remembered all of it. That era had been too emotional to forget. Times were turbulent, but his family had been happy.

Feeling oddly nostalgic, he ushered Maggie into the elevator. They reached the parking structure and climbed into his SUV.

Hours later, they traveled on a country road.

Maggie peered out the window at the barren orchards, the winter wheat fields and the empty pastures going by.

"It's really peaceful here," she said.

"Yeah."

She shifted in her seat and turned to look at him. "It must make you homesick."

"Sometimes." When he reached far enough into the past, he thought, to the years his father and Gwen had still been alive. "But I'm used to the city now. To the traffic and the road noise and all that."

"You've become an urban Indian," she said.

"Maybe, but I haven't forgotten the old ways." He respected what his ancestors believed—that the universe was created for more than just man. Everything had a life force, making a significant contribution to the tangible and intangible world, to the earth and the heavens above. "My dad taught me about the early Cherokee."

"Did he teach you what an early Cherokee wedding was like?" she asked, watching him through her magical eyes.

He almost said no, that his father had never explained a traditional marriage ceremony. But somehow he couldn't lie.

"The wedding takes place in the center of the council house," he explained, "near the sacred fire. A priest prays and the bride and groom exchange gifts. Then they—"

"What kind of gifts?"

"The groom gives the bride venison and a blanket. Nothing a modern girl like you would want," he added, trying to downplay the marriage dare.

"And what does the bride give the groom?" she persisted, undaunted by his comment.

"Corn and a blanket. But she also gives him a black-and-red belt that she made herself, and he puts it on during the ceremony."

"What happens next?"

"They drink from a double-sided wedding vase, then the vase is broken. The broken fragments are returned to Mother Earth, and a white blanket is placed around their shoulders, symbolizing their union. White denotes peace and happiness to the Cherokee."

Maggie sat quietly for a moment. Luke could feel her watching him, so he kept his eyes on the road. He didn't want to think about the wedding he didn't intend to have.

"That sounds like a beautiful ceremony," she said. "I like the idea that both the bride and groom are shrouded in white."

He nodded, then glanced at his shirt, realizing how often he wore black—the color the Cherokee associated with death.

Everything in Luke's world was dark, everything except Maggie Connelly. She was charming her way into his life. And quite frankly, that scared the hell out of him.

He turned onto another country road. "We're almost there," he said. He was bringing Maggie home to meet the only family he had left.

Suddenly that seemed much too significant.

Six

Luke turned into a graveled driveway, then parked beside a cozy old farmhouse. With its flourishing evergreens and Early American charm, it seemed to Maggie too serene to be the location of a kidnapping, yet twenty-seven years before, a child had been taken from there.

She glanced at the house, and for an instant she imagined Gwen kneeling on the porch, playing with paper dolls and a cardboard castle.

Lady Guinevere. Maggie had finally chosen a title for the painting, but she didn't have the courage to tell Luke. He hadn't mentioned the picture since the day he'd first seen it.

"This used to be a dairy farm," he said, interrupting her thoughts. "But that was a long time ago, before my parents bought it."

Rather than respond, she sent him a nervous smile, and

he paused to study her. "You seem uncomfortable. Are you worried about meeting my mom?"

"A little," she answered truthfully.

"You don't have to walk on eggshells around her. She doesn't go to parties or social functions, but she can handle having company at home. She isn't crazy. Agoraphobia is an anxiety disorder not a mental illness."

"I never thought she was crazy. I'm just concerned about making a good impression."

"Really? You? The sister of a king?"

"Yes, me." The heiress the media had manufactured. "I might not live up to her expectations."

He reached for the denim jacket he'd tossed in the back seat. "Are you kidding? She already thinks you're special."

Because I'm a celebrity, Maggie thought. Because I was born a Connelly.

They exited the SUV and walked to the back of the house. Luke unlocked the door and they entered through a service porch.

"We're here!" he called out as they proceeded to the kitchen, where the counters were laden with food.

"Oh, my." A woman in a knit pantsuit bustled around the stove.

Maggie assumed she was the housekeeper since Luke hadn't described his mother as a redhead with a teased and sprayed hairdo.

Luke made an introduction. Her name was Nell. She appeared to be in her midsixties, a former waitress with a husky voice and a quick grin. Maggie liked her immediately.

Nell shook her head, spinning the miniature Christmas ornaments dangling at her ears. "You shouldn't bring a guest through the back door, Luke." She flashed her ready smile at Maggie. "Now, isn't that just like a man? Of course, he's a handsome one, so we'll forgive him."

"You must be talking about my son," a softer voice interjected.

All eyes turned to Luke's mother, who had stepped quietly into the room. Dana Starwind stood tall and thin, with silver-gray hair and a smooth complexion. She looked fragile yet strong, her delicate features set amid stunning bone structure. She must have been breathtaking in her day, Maggie thought.

Maggie moved forward, and with mutual interest, they studied each other.

After a proper introduction, the other woman asked, "Did Luke tell you how much I wanted to meet you?"

"Yes, but I hope you don't believe everything that's been written about me."

"You're a graduate student, earning a double major in business and art."

Maggie's pulse quickened. "That part is true." The part most people ignored. The tabloid pictures of her on a yacht in the south of France usually generated the most interest, particularly since her bikini top had come undone—an accident that had been made out to seem like a deliberate, party-girl striptease.

"Dana's an artist, too," Nell said.

"It's a hobby," Dana corrected quickly. "I paint to keep busy. But I saw your work in a magazine. It's exceptional."

And that, Maggie realized, was the reason Luke's mother had been so eager to meet her. Nothing could have pleased her more. "Thank you. I would love to see your work, too."

"Then come to the living room," Dana said with a tinge of shyness. "Nell insists on framing my paintings."

An array of watercolors depicted scenes from nature—flowers blooming in a formal garden, a bowl of lemons in a patch of sunlight, a stream splashing over shimmering rocks. The snowcapped mountains could have been Switzerland, Maggie thought, the vineyards from France, the row of chestnut trees flourishing on Tuscany soil.

"They're all beautiful," she said. Clearly Dana traveled in her mind, creating the world as she imagined it.

Each soul-inspired painting blended with the country charm of the Starwind home. Farm-made furniture complemented historic antiques. Patchwork pillows decorated a pre–Civil War settee, and an old butter churn sat between two straight-back chairs. The entire setting, Maggie thought, brimmed with magic and warmth.

Yet, the absence of family photos told another story. Pictures of Gwen were still too painful to face.

Maggie glanced at Luke. He sat next to his mother. The affection between them was obvious, but so was the ache they shared.

While they made small talk, Nell swept into the adjoining dining room, clearly enjoying her role as the housekeeper. She filled a buffet table with homemade entrées and colorful side dishes.

Proud as a country peacock, she encouraged everyone to eat. Maggie chose a little bit of everything, knowing the feast had been prepared in her honor.

Luke filled his plate as well. "Nell loves to cook."

As they gathered around a sturdy oak table, Maggie smiled at the redhead. Nell cooked and Dana painted—hobbies that gave the two older women purpose. They seemed like good friends, closer than she had expected them to be.

"Mom and Nell used to work at the same diner," Luke said, as if he'd just read her mind.

"Really?" She shifted her gaze to Dana. "You were a waitress, too?"

She nodded. "But that was forty-five years ago."

"It's also how she met Luke's daddy." Nell fanned herself with a napkin. "Goodness, but was that man a looker."

Dana smiled, her brown eyes shimmering. "I fell instantly in love. Jacob Starwind was a truck driver from North Carolina. He was from the Qualla Boundary, the Cherokee reservation," she clarified. "But he worked for a company that had locations in Winston-Salem, Pittsburgh and Chicago. It was a good-paying job, and he was grateful to have it." She reached for her water and took a small sip. "He traveled all over the United States. And whenever he made a delivery in this area, he'd stop by the diner."

"They caused quite a scandal," Nell put in. "An Indian man and a white woman. This was the fifties, mind you, and interracial relationships were still frowned upon back then."

"That's true." Dana glanced at her longtime friend. "My reputation suffered, but I didn't care. I wanted Jacob more than I ever wanted anything. Nell was the only one who didn't judge me."

Nell waved her hand. "That's because you never judged me." She turned and winked at Maggie. "I had a reputation in those days, too."

"I'll bet you did." She pictured the snappy redhead wearing her uniform a tad too tight and flirting shamelessly with the local farm boys.

"Nell was always around when I was a kid," Luke said.

And she was, Maggie realized, the friend Dana had been visiting when Gwen had been kidnapped.

Dana toyed with a three-bean salad. "Eventually the gossip settled down about Jacob and me. He asked me to marry him and had his route changed so he could live here. It was difficult for him to leave the reservation, but in the old days a Cherokee husband would take up residence with his wife's clan. And since my family lived in Illinois, Jacob thought that was the proper thing to do."

"He must have been an honorable man." Maggie gazed at Luke. "Like his son."

He didn't look up from his plate, but Nell and Dana exchanged a feminine glance. And at that moment, Maggie knew they saw what was in her heart.

Hours later, as they said goodbye, both women hugged her. It was, she thought, the acceptance she needed.

"I'll come back again," she told Luke's mother. Next time they would talk about art and literature and the beautiful places they both loved—the European countrysides Dana painted but had never visited.

The following afternoon, Luke entered Maggie's office. It still seemed strange to see a woman occupying Tom Reynolds's desk. The room smelled like hothouse flowers instead of Tom's ever-constant cigarette smoke.

She looked up and smiled. An oversize cappuccino cup sat next to her Rolodex, and a jade paperweight rivaled the color of her eyes.

"I have an assignment for you," he said. "I want you to ask your family about Gregor Paulus. I'm looking for anything, even the most minor detail, that might give us a better understanding of his relationship with Prince Marc."

"He was my uncle's personal assistant."

"I know. But I haven't been able to zero in on the dynamics of their association. Was Paulus Marc's confidant? Or was it strictly a professional relationship?"

"Do you think Paulus is involved?" she asked. "Do you think he's the Altarian mob contact?"

"He's on my list of suspects." Luke took a seat in one of the leather chairs across from her desk. "But I haven't come up with anything linking him to the Kellys. If he was part of the CD-smuggling scam, then Prince Marc brought him into it."

"Why would Marc do that?"

"I don't know. That's why I want you to talk to your family about Paulus. I just can't seem to get a handle on him."

"No problem." Maggie came to her feet, then crossed to the bar. Dispensing the cappuccino machine, she filled her cup. Next she opened the refrigerator and added a swirl of whipped cream to the hot beverage.

When she returned to her desk, she sat on the edge of it, giving Luke an enticing view of long, shapely legs ending in a pair of wicked-looking pumps.

The intercom buzzed. Maggie leaned across the desk to press the button, and as she did, her skirt rode farther up her thigh. Luke told himself not to stare, but he gathered an eyeful anyway.

"Yes, Carol?"

"Is Luke with you?"

"Yes, he's right here."

"Good. I picked up something on my lunch hour both of you need to see."

Maggie stood, and Carol came into the office carrying a copy of a current supermarket tabloid.

The blonde placed it on the desk. The movie star on the cover didn't mean anything to Luke, but as he scanned the minor headlines, he caught Carol's concern.

Connelly Heiress Obsessed With Private Eye.

The word that came out of his mouth was a quick, vile curse.

The story was on page four, along with several photographs of Maggie and him kissing in the snow. The pictures weren't professional quality, which meant someone in his neighborhood must have snapped them for a lark, and then realized who Luke's companion was. He wondered how much the bastard had sold them for.

"I'm sorry," Maggie said.

"It's not your fault."

"Are you going to sue?" Carol asked.

"No." He dragged a hand through his hair. "It'll blow over."

"I already warned building security to be on the lookout for reporters and cameramen," Carol said, proving her loyalty as a trusted employee.

"Thanks."

She went back to work, leaving Luke and Maggie alone with the tabloid.

Maggie read the article, while he restrained his temper. He wanted to smash his fist into the wall, but he knew behaving like a hothead wouldn't do any good.

"It says I come to your office every day because I can't get enough of you. Supposedly we're carrying on quite an affair."

He blew out a rough breath. The story also described him as the first "older man" she'd taken up with. That made his stomach churn.

"At least they didn't report that I'm helping you on the case. Of course, they would never suspect that. No one thinks I have half a brain, let alone enough intelligence to assist a respected P.I."

"We were kissing, Maggie." Mauling each other, he thought. "That's all they're interested in."

"Then maybe this is a blessing in disguise. In fact, maybe we should start attending social functions together."

"You mean give credence to the trash they printed?"

"I'm in less danger if the Kelly hit man thinks I'm your lover instead of your temporary business partner, right?"

Luke frowned. She had a valid point, but he didn't like the idea of dragging their lives through the mud, even if it created a believable cover for their association. And then there was that marriage dare. "You're not going to use this as leverage, are you?"

Maggie gave him an incredulous look. "You think I'm going to try to win the dare by seducing you in public?"

He shrugged. What did it matter? She wasn't actually serious about marrying him. She'd devised the dare as a challenge, as a creative way to get his attention. And he had accepted it to teach her a lesson, to prove she had no business trying to change him.

"We'll start this evening," she said, reaching for her cappuccino. "You can escort me to an art show I was invited to. I'm tired of staying home every night anyway."

"Fine," he responded, expecting to be bored out of his skull. He appreciated the kind of art he could understand, but there were plenty of wacky sculptures and paintings out there he could never relate to. Luke knew damn well he didn't fit into Maggie's avant-garde world. They didn't belong together, and no amount of phony dating was going to turn them into real-life lovers.

Luke had never drooled over a woman, but this just might be a first.

Maggie's cocktail dress was the size of a postage stamp. The silver fabric shimmered over every lethal curve, exposing a hint of cleavage and more leg than she had the right to own. A sparkling necklace and a pair of stiletto heels completed the killer package.

Even Bruno couldn't keep his eyes off her.

She smiled at Luke. "Are those for me?"

"What? Oh, yeah." He'd forgotten about the roses. Bringing her flowers seemed like the proper thing to do, even on a fake date. He handed them to her and noticed the dress turned her eyes a moonlit shade of blue.

"Thank you." As she walked into the kitchen to retrieve

a vase, her shoes clicked across the floor, as sleek as silver bullets.

Suddenly it was the sexiest, most dangerous sound he'd ever heard.

She returned with a single rose, the stem snapped short. Moving closer to Luke, she pinned the bloodred flower onto his lapel. He felt as if he'd been branded.

"Shall we go?" she asked, reaching for a wrap that matched her dress.

He merely nodded.

She tossed her head. Her hair was long and loose, golden highlights spilling around her face. "We can take my car." She handed him the keys to her Lamborghini. "It's more showy, and we're trying to get noticed tonight, right?"

Minutes later, Luke slid behind the wheel. Maggie owned one of the six hundred and fifty-seven Countach Anniversario models ever made—a vehicle capable of traveling 183.3 miles per hour.

"I like to move fast," she said.

He pictured making fast and urgent love to her. "So do I."

They flew into traffic and reached their destination in record time. The gallery was located in a historic building with multipaned windows and a brick walkway. Inside, lights burned brightly. A winding staircase led to three spacious floors.

Other guests milled in and out of showrooms. A waiter held a tray in front of them, and Maggie accepted a flute of champagne. Luke declined a glass of the bubbly in lieu of a harder drink from the bar. Maggie took his arm and led him to the first display.

A lone statue stood in the center of a stark white room. They moved closer, and he noticed the sculpture depicted a naked woman; her head tipped back, her long, lithe body arched. A bed of rose petals lay at her feet.

Maggie fingered the flower on Luke's lapel. He wanted to pull her tight against him.

The next room showcased a trio of paintings, each more sensual than the last.

"Damn," was the only word he could manage. He couldn't take his eyes off a painting that focused on a woman kissing a man's navel. Only his bare stomach and the waistband of his jeans were visible, making the image mysteriously provocative.

She sipped her champagne. "A nameless, faceless man. He could be anyone."

"Yeah." And Luke was imagining Maggie's mouth on his stomach. "You should have warned me."

"What? That this show is a collection of erotic fine art? It must have slipped my mind."

Like hell, he thought. She'd done it on purpose, and her ploy had worked. Desire gushed through his veins.

But at this point he didn't care. He was going to take what he wanted. Immune to the fact that they were in a public place, he grabbed her by the shoulders and kissed her—hard. So hard he nearly lost his breath.

She kissed him back, and he explored the hot, impulsive sensation, running his hands up and down her dress. Hungry for more, he toyed with the idea of devouring her in one quick bite.

Fast, he thought. He wanted it fast. The way an addict injected a drug or an alcoholic downed a forbidden drink.

And then he realized he was dangerously close to spilling his vodka on the marble-tiled floor.

Pulling back, he stared at Maggie. Her eyes were a fiery shade of blue, her lips still slightly parted. The silver dress reflected sparks of light, like a chandelier casting vibrant rays.

"Don't trick me again," he said. "Don't set me up for another seduction."

"But that's part of enjoying life," she challenged.

And part of the dare, he thought, realizing she had just won the first round. She sent him a triumphant smile, and he had the notion to grab her, to tip her head back and taste her all over again.

"Maggie?" a feminine voice said behind them. "Darling, is that you?"

They both turned. A well-preserved blonde in a black dress clung to the arm of her young, brawny escort.

Instantly, the irony hit Luke. He figured the couple had at least seventeen years between them, just like him and Maggie. Suddenly this game, this dare, seemed morally wrong.

"Delilah." Maggie reached out to hug the blonde. "It's so good to see you."

"You, too." Delilah tilted her head. She wore her hair in an upswept style, showing off the gems at her ears and the jewels at her throat. "You must be the private eye," she said to Luke. "Maggie's handsome obsession."

"That's what the tabloids say."

The blonde laughed. "I have an obsession, too. Let me introduce you to him."

Luke shook hands with the young man and wondered if the guy was receiving stud-service pay or if he dated Delilah for free.

When the couple moved on, Luke drained his glass, swallowing the last of his vodka. Maggie was still sipping eloquently on champagne.

"Delilah is a patron of the arts. She has an amazing collection."

"Of what?" he asked sardonically. "Twenty-five-year-old men?"

She glared at him. "That was her husband."

"And that's supposed to impress me? Some young gigolo marrying a rich divorcée?"

"First of all, Delilah isn't a divorcée. And second, she and Kevin live in an estate *both* of them paid for. She didn't marry him for his body, and he didn't marry her for her money." Maggie looked him straight in the eye. "And since neither one of them can have children, they plan on adopting an orphan from Bosnia."

Luke caught the information right in the gut. He rarely, if ever, misjudged people. It was his business and his nature to look beyond stereotypes. "I'm sorry," he said. "I had no right to insult your friends."

"That's okay. I did the same thing when I met Carol. So I guess we're both guilty of jumping to conclusions."

With a forgiving smile, she took his hand and led him toward another incredibly erotic piece of art, intent on drawing him into her world.

Seven

Maggie's childhood room had been redecorated since her youth, but it still felt like home. French doors led to a balcony that overlooked the gardens. She stared at the view, picturing herself as a child hiding in the maze and pretending to be braver than she was.

"Maggie?"

She turned to the sound of her mother's voice.

As always, Emma Rosemere Connelly was the image of beauty and grace. She wore her blond hair in a French twist, and a strand of pearls accented a classic Chanel suit. Maggie had never seen her mother looking unkempt or frazzled.

"Are you all right?" Emma asked.

She nodded and perched on the edge of the bed. "Did you see the tabloid article, Mom?"

Emma sat in a velvet side chair. "I heard about it, but I certainly wasn't inclined to read it."

"Dad isn't upset?"

"He doesn't intend to confront Mr. Starwind if that's what you're worried about. Luke already called and apologized."

Maggie didn't know whether to be pleased or angry. She appreciated the fact that Luke respected her honor, but she didn't want him apologizing for their relationship or downplaying the emotion between them.

"We already knew that you and Luke were attracted to each other."

She reached for a pillow. "You did?"

"We saw you dancing with him at Rafe and Charlotte's reception. The way he held you, the way you looked at him...well, it wasn't hard to miss."

"I'm in love with him."

"Oh, my." Emma placed a jeweled hand against her heart. "Are you sure? This isn't just one of your impulses, is it?"

"No." She met her mother's gaze with a candid stare. "This is the real thing. And I've never been so frustrated in my life. If we're not snapping at each other, we're fantasizing about tearing each other's clothes off."

"Well, then."

Emma coughed delicately, and Maggie bit back a smile. She never failed to surprise her family with her blatant, if not inappropriate, honesty. "Tell me what it was like when you first fell in love with Dad."

The older woman sighed. "It was wonderful. But it was turbulent, too. Grant was such a dynamic man. So proud, so strong." She fingered a pearl at her ear. "And much too crass for the likes of my family. As you know, my parents were heartbroken, as well as angry, that I didn't marry another royal. I was a princess. It was my duty to form a strategic alliance for my country."

"But instead, you gave up your title and married a rugged American."

"Yes." Emma smiled. "I was headstrong in my youth, too."

"Do you ever regret your decision?" she asked, curious how her mother had coped with the knowledge that her husband had slept with his former secretary. "You and Dad did have some problems."

"I've never regretted marrying the man I love. And our troubles happened long before you were born. A lifetime ago." Glancing at the balcony, Emma paused as though tempering painful memories. "A person has to learn to forgive, to work through the hurt."

"What about your sacrifice?" Maggie asked, trying to envision her mom as a young, headstrong princess. "All those years away from your family?"

"That was the most difficult part. And now, of course, I'm grateful I had the chance to make peace with my father before he died." Five years before, Emma had gone back to Altaria to make amends with King Thomas, bridging the gap between the Connellys and the royal family.

Glancing at the pillow on her lap, Maggie toyed with the lace edge. Her mother must be devastated by Prince Marc's treachery. Maggie had already questioned Emma, as well as other family members, about Marc's association with Paulus. "Luke is going to solve this case."

"I trust that he will," Emma responded. "And I'm also aware that you're determined to help him. That worries me, Margaret," she added, using her daughter's formal name.

"Luke promised Rafe that he would keep me safe."

"I know, but you're so reckless at times. You have to be careful and listen to what Luke says. He isn't just a private investigator. He was a Special Forces soldier. He has experience in these sorts of matters."

"I won't defy him. I just want to be part of this, to make a difference." Maggie tilted her head. "What do you think of Luke, Mom?"

The other woman clasped her hands in her lap. "He's a good man. Your father and I like him."

"Good. I'm glad." She sent her mother a confident smile, even though her heart was beating triple time. "Because sooner or later, I intend to marry him."

The following morning Maggie's car phone rang. She pressed the speaker button. "Yes?"

"It's Carol. Are you on your way to work?"

"Yes." And she was running late as usual. She glanced at Bruno. The dog rode shotgun, staring out the Lamborghini's tinted window. "We should be there in about five minutes." She approached a yellow light and sped through it. "Maybe four."

"Luke's in a foul mood, Maggie."

She checked her rearview mirror, spotted a cop and slowed down. "Why? What's wrong?"

"Another tabloid hit the stands today. And it has Luke fuming."

Shoot. "Thanks for the warning, Carol. I owe you one." She ended the call and proceeded to the office, reminding herself to breathe. Of course Luke was upset. He wasn't used to being in the limelight. He hadn't lived his life under public scrutiny.

"Well, he better get used to it," she told the dog. "Particularly since he's going to marry a Connelly."

Bruno grinned at her, and she patted his head. She'd fed him steak and eggs for breakfast, with a scatter of corn chips on the side. He was adjusting to her devil-may-care lifestyle with ease.

She pulled into the parking lot and wondered if she should have dared Bruno to marry her instead.

The moment she exited the car, a camera flashed its glaring bulb in her face. She squinted at the photographer, a squirrelly little man who touted himself a "royal watcher."

While he continued to snap her picture, she let Bruno out on the passenger side, giving him a subtle command. The big dog bared his teeth. The cameraman jumped back, slipped on a grease spot and fell flat on his rear.

Maggie waved to the "royal watcher" from the parking-lot elevator. Bruno snarled until the door closed.

At the reception desk, Carol had the phone glued to her ear. She gestured toward Luke's office, letting Maggie know he was waiting for her.

She nodded, removed her coat and gloves, then proceeded to the lion's den.

Luke was pacing, so she stood silently, allowing him to stalk the perimeter of his cage, hoping he would get the agitation out of his system.

Finally, he stopped. "A love triangle," he said, spewing the headlines like an expletive.

Maggie unhooked Bruno's leash, but the dog didn't leave her side. "I don't understand. A triangle implies there's a third party."

"It says Claudio and I are fighting over you."

"Really?" She tried not to smile. Claudio Di Salvo, a free-spirited playboy on the international racing circuit, wouldn't dream of fighting over a woman.

Luke stared her down. "Are you still seeing him?"

She managed a casual shrug. "We're still friends, if that's what you mean."

"What kind of friends?"

Maggie took a seat, thrilled that Luke appeared jealous of her former lover. She wanted him to feel possessive of her, to think of her as his. "Are you asking me if I still sleep with him?"

"You know damn well that's what I'm asking."

She crossed her legs, feigning indifference. Bruno, her faithful companion, chose to lie at her feet. "I don't think that's any of your business."

"The hell it isn't. I have a right to know just how much of this article is true."

Maggie picked up the tabloid off his desk and breezed through it. The pictures of her and Luke kissing were plastered across a page, along with a cozy shot of her and Claudio at a casino in Monaco. She read the text, and then went on to check her horoscope. On a whim, she checked Luke's horoscope, too, wondering if their signs were compatible.

Finally, she looked up, meeting his piercing gaze. "Actually, none of it is true, but Claudio won't mind. He gets a kick out of these sorts of things."

"Well, hooray for Claudio."

"Honestly, this is no big deal. My affair with him was quite casual, you know."

"How European of you," he said, his voice tight and cynical. "But if you don't mind, I'd just as soon not hear the details. I've had enough of Claudio for one day."

Because you're jealous, she thought. And you're worried that he was better suited to me.

She closed the tabloid. Claudio had been her first and only lover, and although he had satisfied her physical needs, their relationship had lacked an emotional bond. Maggie craved true intimacy—the kind she hoped Lucas Starwind could give her.

"I don't sleep around," she said, suddenly concerned about his opinion of her. "And I would never pit one man against another."

Luke saw the discomfort in her eyes and realized how

unfair he was being. "Is that how I made it sound?" He leaned forward. She smelled like flowers, like spring on a winter day. "I'm sorry. I didn't mean to blame you. I'm just not used to all of this."

"I know. It's like living in a fishbowl."

He reached out to touch her cheek, felt the softness of her skin. Was he falling for her? he asked himself. This young, beautiful muse?

Yes, he thought, drawing his hand back. He was falling down a mountain. Running headlong into a speeding train. And sooner or later he'd end up with emotional scars. How long could he keep a woman like Maggie interested? How much time would pass before she got bored? Before his graying-at-the-temples appeal wore off?

He went around to the other side of the desk, determined to put a barrier between them. "We better get back to work," he said, forcing himself to focus on business. The Connelly case was going nowhere. Luke had a list of suspects and no substantial leads.

"Did you talk to your family about Gregor Paulus?" he asked.

"Yes." She reached for her briefcase, placed it on her lap and opened it. Glancing at her notes, she said, "I wasn't able to reach Princess Catherine. She's the one who probably knows Paulus the best."

Luke nodded. Princess Catherine, the recent bride of a sheikh, was also Prince Marc's illegitimate daughter. "Where is she?"

"On a holiday with her husband."

"Will she be at the coronation rehearsal?" he asked, knowing Maggie and her family would be traveling to Altaria within the next few weeks.

"Yes. Are you going, Luke?"

"It depends on what happens with this case. I've got

plenty of people keeping an eye on things in Altaria.'' He scrubbed his hand across his jaw, wishing something would turn up. ''Tell me what you learned about Gregor Paulus.''

''Overall, he isn't a very likable man. He's overbearing, so much so that he argues over trivial things. The king intends to fire him after the coronation. Paulus lied about several small domestic matters, and my brother isn't going to put up with that.''

Luke had heard most of this before. ''What about Paulus's relationship with Prince Marc?''

''Prince Marc treated Paulus well, but still considered him an employee, or a servant, if you will. Paulus knew his place, and he never tried to step out-of-bounds where Marc was concerned.''

''So they weren't friends?''

''No.''

''Was Paulus your uncle's confidant?''

''Maybe. No one is sure what they discussed in private. Of course, Princess Catherine might be able to tell us something pertinent, but she isn't available for an interview right now.''

''Then we'll wait.''

''Who else is on your list of suspects?'' she asked.

He conjured a mental image of the names imbedded in his brain. He counted them like sheep before nodding off to sleep each night. ''The security personnel at the Rosemere Institute, the scientists who discovered the cancer virus, the owner of the Altarian textile mill that manufactured the lace. And besides Gregor Paulus, there's a slew of people employed in the royal service who could have discovered that Prince Marc was associated with the mob.''

''But you have a hunch about Paulus?''

''I suppose you could call it that.'' Luke leaned back in

his chair. "What do you think of him, Maggie? What's your gut instinct?"

She blinked, shuffled her notes, then smoothed her skirt. Nervous, he thought. Or embarrassed that she didn't have an opinion of one of their key suspects.

"I never paid much attention to him."

"I see." He brought his hands together, forming a steeple. "And what do you think his observation of you would be?"

"That I'm rich and spoiled. That the only things that matter to me are designer clothes, fast cars and good-looking men."

Intrigued, he watched her hair spill over her shoulders. "Why would he think that about you?"

"Because that's my reputation," she answered simply.

Luke had to admit that her reputation was easy to believe. Or it had been before he'd started spending time with her. Now he didn't know what to think.

"You shouldn't work here anymore," he said.

She frowned at him. "You can't take me off this case. You—"

"I'm not. But you can assist me without coming into the office every day. You're causing too much of a stir. Pretty soon the other tenants are going to start complaining about all the photographers hanging around." And she was, he thought, a nine-to-five distraction he didn't need.

"Take the rest of the day off," he told her. "I'll come by tonight to help you reorganize your home office."

"This isn't fair."

He ignored her protest. "I'll bring your files. I've got plenty of work to keep you busy. You can follow up on Tom's old notes. Maybe he stumbled upon something I missed. Something besides the information that got him killed."

"But I like working here. I like being around you and Carol."

She pouted, and Luke realized how young she really was, how headstrong yet vulnerable. He worried she might cry. He didn't think he could handle that, so he gave her a stern look, hoping it would rile a temper rather than tears. "Don't fight me on this, Maggie."

She made a face at him and grabbed her coat. Outside, the weather turned damp. Suddenly he could hear a gush of rain.

"You're going to miss me, Lucas Starwind. It's going to be boring around here without me."

She dropped her gloves. He picked them up and handed them to her. He didn't doubt for a minute that he'd miss her. And that was exactly why he was shooing her away. He didn't like the idea that she had become so important in his life.

Eight

Maggie told herself not to cry, but as rain pounded against her windshield, tears flooded her eyes. If she lost the dare, she would lose Luke.

Sniffing like a heartbroken teenager, she steered her car down a water-slicked highway. Bruno sat beside her, patient and gentle as a lamb. She couldn't imagine life without the big dog. Or a day without Luke.

Damn him. He was pushing her away, closing himself off, shielding his heart from what he was afraid to feel. And there didn't seem to be anything Maggie could do about it. Except bawl like a baby.

Hours later, she arrived on Dana Starwind's doorstep, dripping with rain and wiping her nose.

"Oh, honey." Dana ushered her inside, then gasped when Bruno tromped in as well.

"He won't hurt you. He's my bodyguard."

"He certainly looks big enough for the job." She paused

to study the rain-sodden pair. "Let's get both of you dried off."

While Dana removed Maggie's coat and wrapped her in an oversize towel, Bruno watched with interest. When the older woman knelt, the dog lifted his paw to shake her hand. She smiled, took his muddy foot and wiped it clean. Like an expectant child, he offered his other paw, then allowed her to go to work on his back feet.

They proceeded to the kitchen where meatballs simmered in a pot of sauce. The scent of garlic, oregano and basil danced through the air. A loaf of Italian bread sat on the counter.

Nell came in from the pantry, took one look at Maggie's red-rimmed eyes and began preparing meatball sandwiches with slabs of mozzarella melting in the center. It seemed as though she believed a home-cooked meal had the power to comfort a saddened heart.

Bruno sat in a toasty corner, sniffing and hoping for his share. But he didn't need to wait long. Nell fed everyone, including the dog.

They gathered around a small fifties-style table in the kitchen, dripping sauce on a vinyl tablecloth and drinking colas spiked with grenadine. It was, Maggie decided, food for the soul.

After their meal she helped the women clean up. There was no automatic dishwasher. They accomplished the task with a sinkful of suds, rubber gloves and two checkerboard-print towels.

No one asked why she had been crying. Instead they welcomed her into a routine that made her feel as if she belonged there. She still sported the chic designer suit she'd worn to the office that morning, but that didn't seem to matter. Maggie was one of them. She was part of Luke's family.

A short while later, while Nell retired in an easy chair with a book, and Bruno dozed on a carpet by the hearth, Dana took Maggie to the room she used as a studio.

A braided area rug padded the floor, and a blank canvas rested on a lone easel, waiting for a stroke of color.

Maggie glanced at the eyelet curtains. And because she felt a softness, a gentleness in the air, she sensed this room had once belonged to Gwen.

Dana crossed to a wood shelf and brought back a handful of tiny figures.

"Luke made them," she said.

Maggie reached for one and studied it. Fine and smooth, the stone carving depicted a howling wolf, its head tipped to the sky. "It's beautiful."

"They're all wolves." Dana held them protectively. "They represent the A-ni-wa-ya, the Cherokee clan Luke's father belonged to. In the old days, the Wolf Clan raised wolves, training the pups like dogs."

"When did Luke make these?"

"Years ago, when he was a boy."

Before Gwen died, Maggie realized. "What was he like back then?"

Dana smiled. "He loved being outdoors. He had a horse named Pepper, and he would ride through the fields, whooping and hollering. He was tall for his age, and his hair was long, just past his shoulders."

Maggie pictured him, the boy who carved wolves, racing in the wind, scents and sounds from the earth stirring his young, vibrant soul. She could even hear his laughter, the freedom that rang from his chest.

"You're the first girl he's brought home since high school."

Startled, Maggie looked up. "I am?"

"Yes." Dana placed the wolves back on the shelf, then

closed Maggie's hand around the one she held, silently telling her to keep it. "I know there have been women in his life, sexual partners, I suppose. But he's never mentioned a name or brought anyone here. I gave up on the idea of becoming a grandmother long ago."

Suddenly the wolf in Maggie's hand felt warm and alive. She brought it next to her heart. "I dared him to marry me."

Now it was Dana's turn to startle. "Oh, my. How did he react to that?"

"He accepted the dare, but only because he doesn't think I can win. I made him promise that he had to marry me if I could make him stop hurting."

Luke's mother glanced at the window. Rain slashed against the glass, pounding in a steady stream. "He doesn't want to stop hurting, does he?"

"No. Your son blames himself for everything bad that's ever happened. He carries the weight of the world on his shoulders."

"Because of Gwen," Dana said softly. "Did he tell you about her?"

"Yes." And she had painted the little girl without knowing it. She had created an image of Gwen with the winged horse that had taken her to heaven.

"Luke loved her so much. He was such a good big brother. He would have given his life for her." The other woman paused and a breath shuddered through her. She met Maggie's gaze, a gray light filtering between them. "But, then, that's what happened, isn't it? Somewhere along the way, he did stop living."

"So did you, Dana."

"I—" Her excuse faded, and she sighed. Twisting her hands together, she glanced at the blank canvas. "You won't give up on us, will you, Maggie?"

"No," she promised. "I won't give up."

Both women stood silently then, listening to the downpour and wishing for a rainbow.

At 12:00 a.m. Maggie entered the parking structure below her loft and saw Luke's SUV. Surprised, she took the elevator to the first floor and unlocked her door, wondering why he was there at this hour and why he'd finally made use of the key she'd given him.

Bruno went in ahead of her and got her attention, leading her to the couch. Luke was sprawled across it, fast asleep. His holstered gun, a weapon that seemed out of place in her artistically designed home, sat on the engraved coffee table.

Maggie moved closer. Luke looked hard and strong, even in repose. His hair fell in an inky-black line across his forehead, and shadows cut across his face, defining his rugged features. His shirt was partially untucked and he'd removed his boots, but his belt was buckled, his jeans zipped. They were an old, faded pair of Levi's, fraying at the seams.

Unable to stop herself, she smoothed his hair.

He jerked and came awake.

"Maggie?" He squinted at her. "What time is it?"

"After midnight."

"Damn." He sat up. "I didn't mean to sleep that long. I just closed my eyes for a second."

"That's okay. What are you doing here?"

"I brought the files by after work, but you weren't here, so I left them." He rolled his shoulders and tucked in his faded denim shirt. "I went home, but when you didn't return my messages, I came back."

She wanted to stroke his cheek, but she knew he wouldn't understand the tender gesture. She kept seeing him as his mother had described him—young and beautifully free. "You were worried about me?"

He shrugged. "I figured you were visiting a friend or

something, but I wanted to be sure. It was raining pretty hard.''

"Why didn't you try my cell?"

"I did. And your car phone, too. You didn't answer."

"Oh." She dug through her purse and flipped open her phone. The battery, as usual, was dead. "I guess I forgot to charge it." And she hadn't thought to check her car phone for messages. She wasn't used to having people fret over her. Her family had accepted her independence long ago.

"You have to be more careful, Maggie."

"Bruno was with me."

"I know. But still, it really bugged me when I couldn't reach you."

She sat beside him on the couch, her heart swelling. "Thank you." She touched his arm and felt the hard-earned muscle beneath his sleeve. "It matters that you care."

He frowned, intensifying the lines at the corners of his eyes. "You're my responsibility until this case is solved."

He couldn't say it, she thought. He couldn't admit that he cared, not even a little.

Maggie watched as he picked up the 9mm, reached behind him and clipped it to the back of his belt. She didn't want to be his responsibility; at least not in the way he meant it. But, then, he was a former Special Forces soldier. It was his nature to keep a level head, to focus on whatever mission he had been given. And at the moment her safety was part of his assignment.

"Will you stay here tonight?" she asked, not wanting to let him go. "You can sleep in one of the guest rooms, and in the morning I'll fix breakfast. I cook a pretty mean omelette."

"No. I can't."

"Can't or won't?"

"It isn't a good idea." He grabbed his boots and shoved

them on. They were as timeworn as his jeans. "Us sleeping under the same roof." He tied the laces on his boots, knotting them twice.

She watched him, imagining his hands on her body, his heart beating next to hers. "I fantasize about you," she said. "When I'm lonely, I touch myself and think about you."

She heard his breath catch, and the reality of her words hit. She had just told him her deepest, most intimate secret. Instantly shamed, she hugged herself for comfort, wanting to die a thousand deaths.

She felt herself blush, knowing two rosy spots colored her cheeks. "I'm sorry. I didn't mean to say that. I—"

He lifted his gaze and slammed straight into hers. Neither moved. They sat, staring at each other, the air between them as jagged as a shard of glass.

Luke's entire body shuddered. He was too shocked, too aroused to think straight. If he didn't leave, if he didn't force his legs to carry him to the door, he was going to drag Maggie into his arms. Push his tongue into her mouth, tear at her clothes, bury himself between her legs.

Deep, he thought. Deep and wet between her legs.

"I have to go." He shot up like a rocket and nearly tripped over the dog, feeling big and boyish and stupid.

"I'm sorry," she said again.

"Don't apologize." He jammed his hands in his pockets and tried to act casual. "People do that. They…you know, fantasize." Flustered, he removed his hands from his pockets, suddenly worried that they would call attention to his distended fly.

"Do you?" she asked, gnawing on her lip.

Luke felt like a sexually starved teenager, a kid too shy to admit that he had normal, healthy urges. "Sometimes. Especially if it's been awhile since I've—" He paused, searching for the appropriate term. When nothing but raunchy words came to mind, he settled on, "Been with some-one."

"Oh." She grabbed a decorative pillow and twisted the tassel. "Has it been awhile?"

Determined to avoid her gaze, he glanced at the wall, then caught sight of the mermaid mural. Cursing to himself, he shifted his gaze again. That erotic painting wasn't helping. "Yeah. It feels like it's been forever."

"For me, too," she admitted.

In the next instant they both fell silent. She hugged the tasseled pillow to her chest, and he glanced at the white-washed floor, trying to think of a way to change the subject.

"I put the files in your office," he managed to say, gesturing to the computer room down the hall.

"Thank you. I'll sort through them in the morning."

"Great. Well, I better go. It's getting late." He checked his watch, then realized he wasn't wearing one. This had to be, he thought, the most awkward, strangely sexual moment of his life. He was still fully aroused, still turned on by what she'd told him.

She walked him to the door. They stammered through a goodbye and, when the elevator descended, he dropped his head against the wall and let out a rough I-should-have-spent-the-night-with-her, she's-all-I'm-going-to-think-about, how-in-hell-am-I-going-to-sleep breath.

Maggie couldn't sleep. She tossed and turned in bed, stared at the ceiling, watched the clock and thought about Luke. The rain had started up again. She could hear it pounding on the roof.

The phone rang, and she nearly jumped out of her skin. Nothing but bad news came in the middle of the night.

She answered the call, fearing the worst.

"Maggie, it's me." Luke's husky voice came over the line. "I didn't wake you, did I?"

"No. Is something wrong?"

"I can't sleep."

She snuggled deeper under the covers. "Me, neither."

Silence bounced between them before he said, "I've never had phone sex, have you?"

"No." She focused on the rhythm of the rain to keep her pulse from running away with her. "Is that why you called?"

"Yeah, but I don't think I'm going to be very good at it."

Did he want her to say something erotic? To start the forbidden game? She wasn't sure what to do. She couldn't exactly tell him what she was wearing. Her flannel pajamas had cartoon characters all over them. They were her silly, cold-weather indulgence.

"I wish you would have stayed here," was the only thing she could think to say. It was, after all, how she felt. She missed him terribly, and now the rain sounded lonely and sad.

"Me, too. But deep down, I know better."

"I haven't made things easy on you," she said, aware of the fire, the fine line between passion and anger, that fueled their reactions to each other. "How many times have I accused you of being with someone else?"

"I would never do that, Maggie. I would never hurt you deliberately."

"Thank you. That means a lot to me." In her heart she knew he was an honorable man, but she needed to hear him say it, to admit in some small way that he cared.

"I was jealous, too," he said. "And things like that never mattered to me before. I've never been in a committed relationship."

"But you should be, Luke. You need someone." You need me, she thought, the woman who loves you, the woman who dreams about you every night. "You should have a wife and children."

His response was quick. Too quick. "I'm not the husband type. And I'd make a terrible dad."

"No, you wouldn't." Maggie could see him holding an infant against his chest, whispering softly in the Cherokee language. The dedicated father, the protective warrior. "A child would be lucky to have you."

"Do you want kids?" he asked, his voice suddenly rough with emotion.

"Yes. But I hadn't given it much thought until I met you." She adjusted the phone. "I want your babies, Luke. Think of how beautiful our children would be." She glanced at the window. She'd left the blinds open, inviting the city lights to filter in, to slash watery hues across the room. "Come over and make a baby with me."

He was silent for a moment, and she knew he was imagining them together, his body spilling into hers.

"We can't let that happen," he said. "You know we can't." He released a heavy sigh. "This is crazy. I'm standing in front of the fireplace at two in the morning, talking about making babies."

It wasn't, she realized, the kind of conversation he'd anticipated. It was deeper, much more intense than he'd bargained for. "I thought you were in bed."

"No. I'm too restless to lie down."

She pictured him, a crackling fire sending golden waves over his skin. In her mind's eye, his chest was bare and frayed denims rode low on his hips. And his hair, that midnight hair, would be tousled from dragging his hands through it.

Her heart went soft. Tough, detached Luke. He'd called

because he needed her, because he couldn't bear to sleep alone. "Climb into bed," she said, wishing she could hold him. "And we'll keep each other company."

"Okay." She heard a smile in his voice. "But you've got to talk dirty to me."

She laughed. She knew he was kidding. At this point, all they would do was cuddle and listen to the rain.

Dawn stole its way into Luke's room, and he awakened with a cordless phone jammed against his ear. He listened for a dial tone and heard nothing but stillness coming from the other line. He was still connected to Maggie's phone, but she was asleep.

What they'd done last night seemed even more intimate than sex. Remaining on the phone had been romance in its purest, most innocent form. And that, he thought as he sat up and shoved off the covers, was dangerous.

"Maggie?" he whispered her name into the receiver, recalling the tender emotion they'd shared.

Come over and make a baby with me.

For an instant last night, he'd been tempted. But then reality had set in, and he knew he couldn't give that much of himself. Nor could he live the rest of his life worrying about keeping his children safe.

"Maggie?" he said her name again. But this time when she didn't respond, he ended the connection, pressing the power button. A shiver sliced through him, and suddenly he felt as if he'd just severed a limb.

No, he told himself. Don't you dare form that kind of attachment to her, that kind of gut-wrenching need.

Luke leaned over and placed the phone on the dresser, and it rang a second later. He didn't answer it, not right away. Preparing to hear Maggie's voice, he sat on the edge of the bed. He caught his reflection in the mirrored closet door, thinking he looked like hell. He'd slept in his jeans, and a shadow of beard stubble peppered his jaw.

Finally he answered the phone. "Hello?"

"Good morning, Lucas."

The woman on the other end of the line was his mother. He cleared his mind, or at least he tried to. Maggie still dominated his thoughts. "Hey, Mom."

"I wanted to catch you before you left for work."

"No problem." He opened the blinds, insisting he wasn't disappointed that the call wasn't from Maggie.

"I'm going to see a doctor," she said.

"Why? What's wrong? Are you sick?"

"It's been twenty-seven years since I've traveled more than a few blocks from my home," she responded. "That's not a particularly healthy way to live."

Stunned by her admission, he rose, carrying the phone into the kitchen. Suddenly he needed a strong dose of caffeine. She hadn't referred to herself as agoraphobic, but she'd said it in her own way.

As he opened a can of coffee, his eyes turned watery. He wanted to blame that uncharacteristic reaction on lack of sleep, but he knew better. "I'm so glad. I want you to be healthy."

"I've made your life so difficult," she said. "You've sheltered me from the outside world, but I can't keep expecting you to do that."

He frowned at the coffee grounds he'd spilled on the counter. "I don't begrudge our relationship. I love you, Mom." Luke was the one at fault, the one who hadn't protected Gwen that day. Dana Starwind had nothing to feel guilty about.

"Oh, Lucas." She made a sad, sighing sound. "I love you, too. And that's why I should have made this decision years ago."

"Don't blame yourself for something you couldn't control."

"I'm through making excuses," she said.

Her voice turned stronger, and he pictured her squaring her shoulders, drawing strength from somewhere deep within.

"There's plenty of help out there," she continued in the same determined voice. "I've seen TV commercials about the medication they give people who feel the way I do. It wouldn't hurt for me to try something."

How long would her bravado last? he wondered. Would she panic later? He had seen her at her frailest, battling the fear and overwhelming grief that kept her chained to the house.

"I'm going to ask Maggie if she'll take me to the doctor. And I think I'll bring Nell along, too. She's been dancing around the house all morning. Prattling about all the things we'll be able to do. Nell wants to go on a cruise. Goodness, can you imagine me on one of those floating casinos?"

He was still stuck on the Maggie part. What had the Connelly heiress said to influence his mother? To make her reevaluate her life?

"I warned Nell not to jump the gun," she said.

She paused, and Luke knew the idea of a cruise made her nervous. Hell, just going to the market made her nervous.

"I'm not fooling myself," she went on. "This isn't going to be easy. I don't expect to turn into a world traveler overnight. Besides, my main concern is attending your wedding."

"What?" He dropped the coffeepot into the sink. The glass carafe bounced but didn't shatter. "I'm not getting married."

"You never know. You might. And I need to prepare for a big social event like that."

Luke's next breath clogged his lungs. When he picked up the coffeepot, his hands were anything but steady.

Come over and make a baby with me.

"I'm not getting married," he reiterated. And he wasn't going to make babies with a woman almost half his age. He was too old and too ornery to be a husband and father. Maggie's affection for him would blow over soon enough. "There isn't going to be any wedding, Mom."

"Oh, my. Listen to yourself, Lucas. You sound more afraid than I do."

He shoved the coffeepot in place, refusing to believe he was basing his decision solely on fear. Even, damn it, if his heart was slamming against his ribs and his mouth had gone unbearably dry.

Nine

The Shaky Shamrock wasn't a dive, but it wasn't a trendy bar, either. It was, in Luke's opinion, an Irish-owned pub that provided a pool table, a stingy dance floor and a working-class environment that normally put him at ease.

Here, he thought, a guy could get friendly with a bottle of vodka and forget his troubles. But only if he wasn't waiting for trouble to arrive.

Where the hell was Maggie anyway? Couldn't she ever be on time?

Luke eyed the clear liquid in his glass, then downed the alcohol and signaled the waitress. One more wouldn't hurt. If anything, it would take the edge off.

Marriage. Babies. He didn't want to think about any of it.

Five minutes later, Luke finished another drink, then sucked on an ice cube. And because he'd heard that sexually frustrated people chewed ice for a diversion, he spit it back into his glass and shelled a peanut instead, hoping no one noticed.

The pub was getting crowded. Couples squeezed onto the dance floor, gyrating to cover tunes played by a local band. Four college-age guys wagered on a rowdy billiards game, laughing above the music. The bartender, a big Irishman with a potbelly and thinning red hair, kept a steady flow of alcohol moving while currency exchanged hands.

Maggie, the recognizable celebrity, came through the door alone—her faithful bodyguard Bruno having been left behind for the evening—and turned every head in the place. And no damn wonder. Beneath a zebra-print coat, she wore a leather dress that made her look capable of handcuffing a man to his bed. Sleek and shiny, the black garment hugged lean curves, stirring even the most staid imagination. And those spiky-heeled boots. Luke envisioned pulling her onto his lap and tangling his hands all through that gorgeous hair.

Talk about needing to chew ice.

He stood, and she walked over to the table. "Am I late?" she asked.

Luke didn't take his eyes off her. "You know you are."

She removed her coat, and he came around to do the gentlemanly thing and push in her chair. And that was when he noticed that her dress was backless.

She turned to look at him. "Is something wrong?"

"No." Nothing that didn't make him a healthy, all-American, hot-blooded male. "You want a drink?"

He could sure as hell use another one. Was it his sixth? he wondered. His seventh? Eighth? Hell, at this point, he didn't care.

"A glass of white wine would be nice," Maggie said, drawing his attention back to her.

Bypassing the waitress, he ordered directly from the bar.

One of the pool players gaped at Maggie, and Luke sent the guy a hands-off stare.

When he returned to the table, she reached for her wine. He sat across from her and watched the way she handled the glass, her fingers sliding up and down the stem. How could someone so young be so damn seductive?

"Do you come here a lot?" she asked.

He shrugged. "Now and then. I don't go out that much."

She looked around. "It's cozy. Kind of rough." Her lips curved into a feminine smile. "I like it."

He guzzled his drink and went after a handful of peanuts. Cozy and rough was the way he wanted to paw her right now. He knew she wasn't wearing a bra. He'd gotten a good look at her naked back and the intriguing shape of her spine.

"So what's on your mind, Luke?"

Sex, he wanted to say. As much of it as I can get. "The case."

She scooted her chair closer to the table. Vintage rock blared from the amplifiers, filling the room with strumming guitar licks, a thumping bass and the pounding of a rhythmic drum. He wondered how she'd react if he asked her to do a private strip show for him tonight. Slide down a metal pole, the whole bit.

"Well?" she asked.

He wanted a lap dance, too. One of those slow, sultry—

"Luke? What's going on with the case?"

"Maybe we should discuss it outside." Where he could inhale a strong gust of city air. Gasoline fumes and factory smoke ought to clear his head right up.

A bit bleary-eyed, he grabbed his jacket. He was drunk and horny, and she was dressed like a dominatrix and sipping a ladylike glass of wine. The odds, he decided, weren't in his favor.

Maggie stood, and Luke helped her with her coat. Once

they were outside, he scanned the parking lot for his SUV. Finding it right where he'd left it, he leaned against the hood. Amber streetlights cast a buttery glow, softening the December night. A damp chill nipped the air. He blew a breath just to see it fog and disappear.

Maggie eyed him speculatively. "How many have you had, Luke?"

"I lost count awhile back, but I remember what I was supposed to tell you about the case. The guy who owned the Altarian textile mill died. Keeled over from a heart attack."

Long, loose hair tumbled around her face. She batted at the breeze-ravaged strands impatiently. "Are you sure he wasn't murdered?"

"Positive. And this really sucks, because he was one of our prime suspects. Those CDs were smuggled out of his mill."

"What about his employees? Could one of them be tied to the mob?"

"It's highly unlikely. We did background checks on all of them. Nothing surfaced, but we didn't expect much. They're just working-class folks."

She slipped her hands in her pockets. Her coat billowed in the wind, snapping like a faux-fur flag. He knew she favored those fake animal prints. She wasn't the sort who went after real fur, even if she could afford it.

"And that's it?" she asked. "That's why you asked me to meet you here?"

"Yep."

"We could have done this over the phone."

Oh, sure. The phone. Where he'd spill his guts about how much he needed her. Or admit that he didn't want to fall asleep without hearing her voice. "Bars are safer."

"For whom?" she asked, taking his keys away.

For guys who are trying to remain single, he thought. "Where's the Lamborghini?" He swept the lot for her vehicle. "I like your car."

"I took a cab. I usually do when I meet a date." She nudged him into the passenger side of the SUV.

Well, hell. He deserved to get his ass kicked, he supposed. She'd been expecting a pleasant night on the town. A little dancing, a little kissing, some warm conversation. "Crummy date, I guess."

"I've had better." She got behind the wheel and started the engine.

He closed his eyes. This was proof, he decided, that he'd make a rotten husband. Proof that he wasn't father material.

Or maybe, he thought, trying to humor himself, this proved that Maggie Connelly was the kind of woman who drove a levelheaded man, some poor unsuspecting sap like Lucas Starwind, to drink.

Three days later Luke and Maggie fixed dinner together in his kitchen. He browned hamburger meat for the tacos, and she diced tomatoes and onions, her eyes watering from the latter.

Luke would never forgive himself for getting drunk the other night. He had no right to do that while Maggie was still in his care. His inebriated state could have put her in danger. What if Rocky Palermo had shown up? How effective would Luke have been against the hit man?

"I'm sorry," he said.

She blinked through the onion-tears. "For what?"

He resisted the urge to dab her eyes. "For the crummy date the other night."

"Oh, Luke. How many times are you going to apologize for that? You deserved to let off a little steam."

Not if it meant putting her in danger, he thought. "I won't do it again. I won't put you in a position to look after me."

"You're making too much of it. All I did was drive you home. You managed to get yourself to bed."

Where he'd conked out soon enough. "I'm still sorry."

"No problem." She scooped the onions into a bowl. "Do you want to hear about what happened with your mom?"

"Yes. Please." He turned the burner down a notch. Chili spices rose in the air, filling the kitchen with a south-of-the-border flair. Maggie had taken his mom to the doctor earlier that day. He hadn't pressed her for details, but he was hoping she would supply a few.

Maggie went to the refrigerator and removed a head of lettuce. "The doctor gave Dana a prescription for an anti-depressant. He explained that some antidepressants are effective in controlling anxiety disorders. The key is finding the right one for her."

"So it's a hit-and-miss kind of thing?"

Still holding the lettuce, she leaned against the sink. "More or less. But he also recommended group therapy. She needs to interact with others who are going through the same thing." Maggie sighed. "You wouldn't believe how many people are afflicted with social phobias. Housewives, executives, movie stars. Some people, like your mom, become housebound, while others appear to function normally when they're actually panicking inside."

Luke nodded. He knew his mom had faked her way through it at first, hiding her fears from him. "What a hell of a way to live."

"Dana is bound and determined to get through this, to do whatever she can to face the world again. And she knows it's not going to be easy. She's not expecting miracles. The toughest part for her will be going places alone. She's relied on you and Nell for so long—"

"I enabled her, didn't I?" he cut in, his stomach clenching.

Maggie met his gaze. "She needed you, and you were there for her. That's not enabling someone. That's loving them." She blinked, her eyes still watery. "You did the only thing you knew how to do, Luke. You protected her."

"But it wasn't enough. I didn't insist that she get help."

"You can't force someone to get help. They have to be willing. And in spite of group therapy and medication, your mom still might suffer from this disorder. There's no guarantee that all of her fears will go away."

But at least now she has a chance, he thought. Because of Maggie—a twenty-two-year-old girl with a heart the size of Texas. He stepped forward. "Thank you for caring."

She set the lettuce down and reached for him. He took her in his arms and guided her head to his shoulder. She felt soft and warm. He stroked her hair and let himself enjoy the luxury of holding her.

Maggie looked up at him, and Luke's pulse tripped. She didn't fancy herself in love with him, did she? She was still young enough to confuse lust with love, still rebellious enough to want a man who was no good for her.

Suddenly the marriage dare didn't seem like a game.

Did it matter? he asked himself. This wouldn't last, not for either one of them. He was too old and set in his ways to get wrapped up in a woman, and she was too young and free to saddle herself with a hard-boiled P.I. forever. She would get over him in no time.

Stepping back, he released her, grateful they hadn't given in to the urge to sleep together. That, he decided, would complicate things, forming a physical attachment they didn't need.

He turned to stir the meat, giving himself something to

do. He would win the dare and that would be the end of it. Midnight on New Year's Eve would come soon enough.

She might be a rich, impulsive Cinderella, but he sure as hell wasn't Prince Charming.

"Do you want me to grate the cheese?" he asked, trying to slip into a casual, meaningless conversation.

"We bought the kind that's already grated."

"Oh, that's right. I forgot." He wasn't used to shopping with someone else or spending so much time with a woman. "I'll set the table." He grabbed the plates and silverware and carried them into the dining room.

Standing in front of the window, he gazed out. Dusk settled in the sky. Rain drizzled on and off, leaving moisture in the air. The neighbor's roof twinkled with strings of holiday lights. Luke turned to glance at his tree, then saw Maggie standing behind him, placing a tray of taco fixings on the table.

"It's beautiful," she said.

He knew she meant his Christmas tree. "Thanks." He'd decorated it with leather-wrapped feathers, hand-engraved silver conchas and strands of turquoise beads. The Indian ornaments reminded him of who he was and where he'd come from. In spite of his urban lifestyle, he never wanted to forget that he had Cherokee blood running through his veins.

"Do you ever go to the reservation to visit your father's family?" she asked.

"Not as often as I would like." Because he had gotten so involved with the city, with the high-profile cases that absorbed his time. "My grandparents are gone, but I still have some distant relatives there." People he barely knew, he realized.

"I'll bet the land is breathtaking."

"It is," he responded, picturing the serenity of the Qualla

Boundary. The rolling pastures, the high meadows, the winding streams. "It's the gateway to the Great Smoky Mountains. It's prettiest at dawn, when the sun shines through the mist."

"I'd love to see it someday. I've never been to North Carolina." Maggie smiled, and he wondered why he felt lonely all of a sudden. Was he missing her already? The enchanting Cinderella he couldn't claim?

A few minutes later Luke and Maggie sat down to dinner. Halfway through their meal the phone rang. He got up to answer it. And then his pulse jumped.

The man on the other end of the line was one of his contacts in Altaria. Finally, they had a lead on the Connelly case.

He hung up the phone and returned to the table. "I'm leaving for Altaria in the morning," he said. "The chief of security at the Rosemere Institute is on the verge of a breakdown. He's ready to crack."

"And you're going to be there when he does."

"Damn straight."

Maggie met his gaze head-on. "I'm going with you."

Her eyes, he noticed, flashed like emeralds. He knew there was no point in arguing, in insisting that she fly over next week with the rest of her family, who would be arriving for the coronation rehearsal. Maggie was determined to remain by his side, to help him solve the case. And that meant getting on a plane with him tomorrow.

"Fine, but Bruno is coming along, too." Luke wasn't about to let Maggie accompany him without her bodyguard. Of course, that wasn't a problem. Altaria didn't quarantine dogs and cats from America, as long as the proper veterinary certificate was provided, and Bruno's medical records were in perfect order. "Just remember, when we get there, I'm in charge. Whatever I say goes."

She agreed, and he reached for his water, promising himself he would do anything, absolutely anything, to keep her safe.

The jet was equipped with everything money could buy—a luxurious living room, a fully stocked bar, sleeping quarters adorned with silk sheets and downy pillows. Maggie sipped a glass of plum wine and nibbled on sushi. She was used to traveling in style, particularly when en route to Altaria. The remote island was only accessible by yacht or private jet as the airstrip was too small to accommodate commercial flights.

She glanced at Luke, who sat beside her on an Italian sofa. Studying his notes, he seemed unfazed by their luxurious surroundings. Then again, he was an experienced flyer and this was, in spite of its glamorous trappings, still a plane.

Bruno yawned from a cozy corner, and Maggie smiled. They made a compatible trio.

Luke looked up. "I hope the security chief has plenty to say. We need a break in this case."

"Especially since one of our prime suspects just died," she said, thinking about Cyrus Koresh, the man who had owned the Altarian textile mill. "Are you sure we don't have anything linking Cyrus to the Kellys?"

"Nothing but the fact that the CDs were smuggled in lace shipments from his mill. He didn't have a record or any known criminal activity. Of course, he was ambitious as hell."

"He must have socialized with someone in the mob," she put in, reaching for a vegetable roll.

"He belonged to the same country club as Gregor Paulus. It could be a coincidence. Plenty of prestigious Altarians belong to the club, but my gut tells me that Paulus is the one who brought Cyrus into this mess.'' Luke stretched his legs. ''You know what the ironic part is? Cyrus's wife died from cancer.''

''Really? Then why would Cyrus agree to smuggle a cancer virus onto the black market?''

''I don't think he knew what was on those CDs. Someone offered him a chance to make some cold hard cash, and he took it.''

''And now he's dead.''

Luke nodded. ''He already had a weak heart, and the stress from the smuggling scheme probably did him in. Whoever else is involved in this must have told him that your brother Rafe discovered what was going on.''

''Which meant Cyrus would be under suspicion.''

''Exactly.''

''The Royal Guard don't know about the cancer virus, do they?'' she asked.

''No. They're aware that files were stolen from the Institute, but they don't know those files contained a potential biohazard. The king thought it was best to keep quiet about that. He didn't want to create a state of panic. We can't afford any leaks.''

And with good reason, Maggie thought. They weren't just going after the mob; they were trying to save the world from biological warfare. ''What do you think the bad guys are doing?''

''Besides dying from heart attacks? Lying low, I would imagine. Or falling apart like the security chief at the Institute.''

''I'm still worried about Daniel,'' she said, recalling the assassination attempt that had been made on his life.

''The king is being protected by the Royal Guard.''

''I know.'' She finished her wine, then managed a reminiscent smile. ''It still seems strange to think of Daniel as a king.'' She remembered her oldest brother as an all-American teenager, slipping past the Connelly cook to swipe a drink from the milk carton, and now he was ruling a nation, a devoted wife by his side.

''You're the one I worry about,'' Luke said as he placed his notes back into a leather briefcase. ''It's dangerous for you to be working with me, Maggie.''

''I'll be fine.'' She had two protectors—a big, burly dog and a former Special Forces soldier. ''How long were you in the military?'' she asked, envisioning Luke as a young, passionate warrior.

''Ten years.''

''Did you enlist when you were eighteen?''

''Yes. I thought about going into law enforcement when my tour ended, but I changed my mind.''

She sensed he had become a P.I so he could investigate unsolved crimes, helping families who needed closure. And somewhere along the way, his skills had led him to high-profile cases.

''We've got a long day ahead of us, Maggie. You should try to get some rest.''

''I am sleepy.'' From the wine, she suspected. She glanced at the bedroom compartments, but decided to nap right where she was. Reclining on the couch, she put her head on Luke's lap and gazed up at him.

With a gentle caress, he stroked her cheek. She imagined unbuttoning his shirt and sliding her hands all over that massive chest.

He toyed with her hair, and a heated shiver slid down her spine.

''Close your eyes,'' he whispered.

Dreamy, Maggie snuggled against his body. But when she turned her head to get more comfortable, she heard Luke suck in a rough breath.

The side of her face was nestled against his fly, and suddenly he was aroused.

That makes two of us, she thought as she drifted into a sweet, sensual sleep.

Ten

Dunemere, the Rosemere family's beach house, faced a rugged coastline. Luke and Maggie stood on a balcony and watched the ocean rise into foaming waves. He thought about the mermaids Maggie had painted and decided that if the sea creatures existed, they would choose to frolic in Altarian waters.

The island, with its sparkling white sand, swaying palm trees and jagged mountains, was indeed a sight to behold.

"I better get ready." Luke turned and entered a suite decorated in chintz, warm woods and mellow pastels. Maggie's suite connected to his, an unlocked door the only barrier that separated them at night.

Moonlit nights, he thought, lulled by the sea.

Maggie sat on the edge of his bed, and he cast her a curious look. "What are you doing?" he asked.

"Nothing," she responded a little too innocently.

Luke knew damn well she was waiting around to see if

he'd strip in front of her. He removed a dark suit from the closet and hung it on a wooden valet. "Scram, little girl." He shooed her away with a dramatic gesture. "Go raid the cookie jar or something."

"Very funny, old man."

They both laughed, and for the first time since they'd met, their age difference seemed almost insignificant.

Almost, he reminded himself. Seventeen years was nothing to scoff at.

She rose, came toward him, grabbed his shoulders and kissed him smartly on the mouth. "Good luck with the security chief," she said.

"Thanks." It took every ounce of willpower he owned not to toss her onto the bed and ravish the hell out of her. She wore a filmy dress that flowed around her like a sheer curtain. He assumed she had some sort of flesh-colored bodysuit on beneath it. The naked illusion was enough to drive him mad.

He watched her walk to the door that divided their rooms. And once she was gone, he let out the breath he'd been holding.

Less than an hour later Luke was seated across from Rowan Neville, the security chief at the Rosemere Institute. The office was clean and organized, with a large desk and metal file cabinets. Nothing appeared to be amiss, nothing but the man himself.

Neville smoked nervously, lighting one cigarette after another. His graying blond hair framed a ruddy, wind-burned face. His tie was so tight, he looked as if he might choke.

Luke eyed him from across the desk. He had been informed that Neville quit smoking twenty years ago. Yet here he was, employed at a cancer-research facility and putting himself at risk for the disease.

Luke presented a document with the royal crest. "The

king sent me here to discuss the Genome Project with you," he said, referring to the name of the research that had accidentally created a virus.

Neville flinched, then took another drag, inhaling as if his life depended on tobacco, tar and nicotine. "The scientists would know about that. You can speak to them."

"The king wanted me to talk to you. He's had someone watching you, Rowan, and he's curious about your odd behavior." Luke sat back in his chair, creaking the leather. He studied the other man, keeping his expression blank. "You've rushed out of the office early every day this week. Why the hurry to get out of here?"

"I needed to get home to my family."

"Why?"

After Neville stamped out the cigarette butt, he fidgeted with the empty pack, clearly craving another. "Because last Saturday I saw the man who threatened to kill them."

Luke's heart leaped to his throat, but he didn't move a muscle. "What man?" he asked.

"The one with the scar." Neville touched his neck, drawing with his finger the scar by which Rocky Palermo was known. "He forced me to do what I did. They needed me, you see. I helped design the security system, and I was able to alter it. No one has clearance to enter the lab at night, not even the scientists."

Luke finally moved, leaning toward the desk. "But you rigged it so someone could get into the lab?"

"Yes. There were two men. One kept me at gunpoint, and the other worked in the computer room. This happened on ten different occasions. The archived data they were after wasn't stored in the same computer. They had to keep coming back, checking different files."

"Give me a description of them," Luke said. "Every detail."

"I can't. They always wore ski masks. I never saw their faces."

"But you saw the man with the scar?"

"Yes, but only a few times last year when all of this first started. He wasn't one of the masked men."

"How can you be sure?"

"Because he was wider than they were. Broader in the shoulders."

Luke scrubbed his hand across his jaw. Either Rowan Neville was a skilled liar, covering his tracks by pointing the finger elsewhere, or he was truly running scared, fearing for his family's safety. "But you saw the scarred man last Saturday?"

He nodded. "At the pier. I was with my children." Pausing, Neville took a breath. "He had a mustache and longer hair, and he wore a turtleneck sweater, so I couldn't see the scar. But the way he was built, the way he walked, I knew it was him." The security chief frowned. "I know it sounds crazy that I recognized a man who didn't look the same, but he threatened my children. That's something a father doesn't forget."

It didn't sound crazy, Luke thought. Rocky often appeared in disguise, but his muscles and cocky stance were hard to miss. Then again, Neville was in a panicked state. He could have mistaken another bodybuilder-type for the hit man. "Did he see you?"

"Yes, but I turned away quickly. He didn't follow me. He was with another man. They were talking quietly."

Luke showed Neville some photographs. The security chief identified Rocky Palermo instantly, but when Luke presented a picture of Gregor Paulus, Neville studied it for a while. "This could be the other man who was at the pier. He was tall and thin like this, but he wore a hooded jacket and dark glasses. It looks like him, but I can't be sure."

Luke decided he would get his computer tech to enhance

the photographs of Palermo and Paulus, creating images of
them in the manner Neville described. ''I'll be in touch,''
he told the other man. ''This is a private investigation. For
now I'm the only person you'll be dealing with.''

Neville fidgeted with the empty cigarette pack once again.
''I'm still worried about my children. And now that I've
told you what I know, they might be in more danger. Will
you speak to the king about protecting my family?'' he
asked, his voice edged with what sounded like genuine fear.

''Yes,'' Luke responded solemnly. He knew Rowan Neville had two rosy-cheeked little girls. ''I will.''

Two days later Luke and Maggie shared dinner in Luke's
suite, a meal provided by a maid—a woman who had been
a loyal Dunemere employee for years. Nonetheless, Luke
had investigated the domestic staff, including the maid. She
and the others had turned up clean, but Luke continued to
sweep their suites for bugs just the same. No one, in his
opinion, was above reproach.

Silent, he toyed with his fork. He'd misjudged the man
who had killed his sister, and Gwen had paid for Luke's
mistake. He would never take anyone at face value again.

''Don't you like the food?'' Maggie asked.

He glanced at his plate. The meal, consisting of maple-
glazed salmon, sautéed chanterelles and cream biscuits, was
fit for royalty. And that, somehow, reminded him of Gwen
and her cardboard castles.

''It's great,'' he responded.

''How would you know? You've barely tasted anything.''

That, he supposed, was true. He'd picked at the spinach
and lentil salad, but he'd bypassed the wild-rice griddle
cakes relished with golden caviar and sour cream. Forcing
himself to focus on his meal, he cut into his salmon. Now
wasn't the time to think about his dead sister.

The fish practically melted on his tongue. He moaned, and Maggie smiled.

"It's almost better than sex, isn't it?"

Luke laughed. Trust Maggie to make him feel better. "Almost," he agreed.

"I guess you've never gotten orgasmic over food before," she said, teasing him.

"No. I can't say that I have." He took another bite, and suddenly the mood shifted. What seemed like an innocent meal was now laced with more than the flavor of maple glaze and peppered cream.

A fire blazed in a gilded fireplace, and outside, the wind howled a haunting melody. Luke sensed the ocean was rising, crashing wildly upon the shore.

Over the candlelit table Maggie met his gaze. Her eyes shimmered like jewels. Muse magic, he thought. The lull of enchantment.

Unable to stop himself, Luke glanced at the bed, knowing Maggie would lie with him if he asked her to.

Heat shot through his veins, as blinding as the fire. He grabbed his water and did his damnedest to douse the flames. If he took Maggie to bed, the addiction would set in, and he would never want to let go.

And that, he thought, as the iced liquid slid down his throat, scared the hell out of him.

"I need to brief you on what's happening with the case," he said.

"Oh, of course." She blinked, as though waking from a fog. "That's why we agreed to dine in your suite."

He nodded. They needed to speak privately, to make certain they weren't overheard. "Rowan Neville identified Rocky in the altered photograph, but he wasn't able to identify Paulus." Luke sat back in his chair. "Let me rephrase that. Neville thought the altered picture of Paulus looked 'a lot' like the man who was with Rocky at the pier. But he wasn't a hundred percent sure.''

"It's the only lead we have, Luke. None of your other suspects could be confused with Paulus. You know it was him.''

"Most likely, yeah.''

"Most likely?'' she challenged. "Did you talk to my brother about this?''

"You mean the king? Yes, I did. And he agreed that we should keep a close eye on Paulus.'' Luke held up a finger to stop Maggie's protest. "We don't have a positive ID on him. Neville can't testify that he saw Gregor Paulus with Rocky Palermo. Hell, his identification of Rocky isn't even airtight. The hit man was in disguise.''

"So we're just going to sit around and wait?''

"Not exactly.'' Luke scooped a forkful of the chanterelles into his mouth. He wasn't a mushroom connoisseur, but they were damn good. "The king suggested that we devise some sort of sting operation.''

"Really?'' Her eyes all but glittered. The muse magic had returned with a vengeance. "We're going to trap Gregor Paulus?''

"Figuratively speaking. It won't be you and me pulling this off. It will involve an undercover agent.''

Her eyes dulled. "So what's the plan?''

"I haven't worked out the details yet. I'm kicking around the idea of baiting him with a potential buyer for the pirated files. As far as I can tell, those CDs haven't turned up on the black market. Their hacker is probably trying to crack the encryption code. Those files aren't worth nearly as much in code, but at this point Paulus would probably welcome a quick, painless sale.''

"Are you sure he even has the CDs?'' she asked. "They

were shipped to Chicago and hidden somewhere by the Kellys.''

''After the Kellys were busted, Paulus probably sent Rocky after them. They wouldn't have taken the chance of leaving them there.''

Luke finished his meal, then eyed the dessert on a nearby serving tray. Deciding to indulge, he reached for a parfait glass and tasted the tapioca and cranberry swirl. Pleased, he made a mental note to compliment the chef.

Maggie sat back in her chair and gave him a serious look. ''We don't need an undercover agent,'' she said. ''I can handle the sting operation.''

He nearly choked on the pudding. ''Excuse me?''

''Think about it. I'm perfect for the job.''

Before he could respond, she continued, ''I'll convince Paulus that I have a potential buyer, but I want in on the deal.'' She leaned forward a little. ''And here's the beauty of it. Paulus has access to some of the CDs, and I have access to the rest. Plus I can get ahold of the encryption program. Together we can sell all the files and make a fortune.''

''And why would he believe that you're on the level?'' Luke shook his head. ''Hell, Maggie, you're practically living with me. The whole world thinks we're lovers. And Paulus knows damn well that I'm investigating this case. He's not an idiot. They killed your grandfather, your uncle, my partner. We're knee-deep in this.''

''And that's exactly why it will work. I have a wild reputation. Like Prince Marc,'' she added. ''The media used to compare me to him. And he was part of the smuggling scam.''

''He owed the mob money. You're a twenty-two-year-old artist with a trust fund.''

''For your information, I won't have access to my trust

fund until I'm thirty.'' She flipped her hair over her shoulder. ''And I can play up that angle. I can say that I need more than the petty cash my stingy family tosses my way. Paulus can skip town after we unload the CDs, and I can defy my parents with my own money, pulling the wool over their eyes in the process.''

Luke couldn't believe what he was hearing. ''What about your relationship with me? How are you going to explain that away?''

She sent him a seductive look. ''I've been using you to get access to the CDs. And, of course, you've fallen prey to my charms.''

He grabbed his water and took a swig. Did she realize the danger she would be putting herself in? People they cared about were dead. Rowan Neville's innocent children had been threatened. Armed guards were protecting the king. And Maggie wanted to walk headfirst into a hornet's nest, with nothing but her youth and feminine wiles. ''Get this ridiculous scheme out of your head right now. I won't consider it, not even for a second.''

She pushed away from the table, rattling the dishes. ''I know I can make it work.''

Luke stood and came toward her. She stared at him defiantly, with her head held high, her chin thrust forward.

''It's a good plan,'' she said. ''And if you helped me refine it, we could catch Paulus.''

''It's dangerous,'' he countered. ''And even if I thought Paulus would fall for it, I wouldn't let you do it.'' Damn it. He cared about her, more than he could say. What would he do if something happened to her? How could he go on?

''That isn't—''

''Don't say another word.'' Frustrated, he backed her against the wall, silencing her argument. And then he realized how close they were. Their faces were inches apart, their bodies almost brushing.

She was still angry. She hissed like a cat, and he lost control. Tugging her head back with her hair, he kissed her, catching her startled gasp as he covered her mouth.

She clawed, then rubbed against him, bumping his zipper with grinding hips. Their tongues mated desperately, and all of his fantasies crashed and tumbled in his brain. Making love to her on the shore, both of them rolling frantically over the sand. The striptease he'd imagined when he'd gotten drunk. The hot, gritty lap dance. He wanted all of that and more.

Ending the kiss, he shackled her wrists in his hand and held her arms above her head. He knew he should step back, release her, kill the urge to tear off her clothes. Maggie Connelly was trouble. She messed with his emotions. She challenged his heart. And she was too young, he thought. Too reckless. Too free.

She met his gaze, her eyes flashing. She looked like a vixen, hot and ready, her hair falling like rain.

"Do it," she said. "Take what you want."

He knew she was baiting him, taking his weakness and using it against him, but suddenly he didn't give a damn.

The need was too strong.

Her dress was red silk, adorned with a row of tiny, jeweled buttons. Luke grabbed the collar and pulled the fabric. Buttons popped as the garment tore, exposing a bra nearly the same color as her skin.

He kept tearing until he saw her panties. She wore a garter belt and hose, and the sultry lingerie turned him on even more. It was as if she knew, as if she'd been preparing for this moment since the night she'd asked him to dance. The inevitable seduction. The unholy surrender.

"Take everything off," he told her. "I want to watch you

undress.'' And then he wanted to ravage her, to make her come, to feel her melt in his arms.

She removed the tattered dress, then unhooked her bra, letting it fall to the floor. When she touched her nipples, Luke's entire body trembled.

Anxious and aroused, he watched. She discarded her shoes, a pair of red leather pumps with spiked heels. The garter belt and hose came next. And after she took off her panties, she slid her hand between her legs. But only for second. For one wild, erotic second.

Luke wasn't in the mood to wait, to play a slow, sexual game. This fantasy was unbridled and swift.

He dropped to his knees, grabbed her hips and pulled her against his mouth.

She bucked on contact, but she wasn't shy. She dragged her hands through his hair and encouraged him to taste her, rubbing and making throaty little sounds.

Young. Free. Reckless.

Licking and kissing, he teased her with his tongue, absorbing the slick, womanly flavor. He knew she was close. He could feel the moisture, the heat, the tangle of electricity.

He looked up at her and saw that she looked back at him. ''Luke.'' She breathed his name, and suddenly her eyes glazed.

He intensified each intimate kiss, and she climaxed, shuddering violently. He kept his mouth there, tasting her release. And when her limbs went molten, he rose to catch her so she could fall gently into his arms.

Maggie felt as if she were floating. And then she realized Luke was carrying her to bed. She kissed him, brushing his lips softly.

''Sometimes when I look at you, I have to remind myself to breathe,'' he said. ''You're all I think about.''

Still dazed, she blinked. She hadn't expected such romantic words, not when he'd just driven her to madness.

She touched his face, skimming her fingers over those rugged features. "You're my lover now." My heart, she thought. The man I love.

He pushed the quilt away and placed her on the sheet. It was cool and inviting against her skin. When she reached for him, he shook his head.

"Not yet," he said, nipping her bottom lip as he kissed her. "We need protection." Luke headed for the bathroom, and Maggie smiled.

Naked and aroused, she scooted against the headboard, feeling delightfully wicked. The lights were on, and the table was cluttered with discarded dishes. Yet the setting seemed perfect.

Luke returned with his shaving kit. He rifled through it, secured a foil packet and placed it on the nightstand. Maggie watched as he undressed hastily, tossing his shirt onto the floor. When he unzipped his trousers, she pulled him onto the bed and they tumbled over the sheet, kissing and dragging off his pants and briefs.

His body boasted power and strength. Sliding her hands over broad shoulders, she followed the ripple of muscle down his stomach to stroke his sex.

He was unbelievably hard, with a bead of moisture pearling at the tip. She lowered her head and kissed him there, tasting the saltiness with her tongue.

His stomach muscles jumped. "Don't do that," he warned.

Maggie didn't listen. Stroking him, she took him in her mouth. In sudden surrender, he lifted his hips and said something unintelligible—a groan, a prayer, a curse—she couldn't be sure. But it didn't matter. Tonight he was hers. Every rough plane, every raw, rugged inch.

He didn't let her claim him for long. He was, she realized, much too eager to engage in the final act. To make love. To join with her.

Luke tore into the condom, sheathed himself and nudged her thighs apart, taking control once again. She let him have what he wanted. She gave willingly—her body and her heart.

He was tender yet rough. Anxious yet somehow patient. He pleasured them both, thrusting deep and then withdrawing, over and over, heightening the sensation. She arched to meet him as he tongued her nipple. And those hands, those skilled soldier's hands, were everywhere, sending slow, dreamy shivers over her skin.

"I don't want this to end," he said. "I want to be inside you forever."

He spoke of sex, but she told herself it was love. She needed so desperately for him to love her.

She could hear the ocean, like a seashell against her ear. Or was it her pulse pounding at her throat? He pressed his forehead to hers, and for a moment the world stilled. There was nothing but them. Lovers who could have risen from the sea.

Overwhelmed, Maggie kissed him. She longed to know his heart, to heal his spirit. This beautiful man, she thought, with the dark eyes and the dark, reclusive soul. Emotion, hers and his, swirled like a mist. She could feel it rise and float over them, a haunting they couldn't see.

They clasped hands, and he increased the rhythm.

Deeper. Stronger.

The maddening, lethal rhythm. The explosive heat.

This was more than sex, she told herself as her body quaked. So much more, she whispered as Lucas Starwind threw back his head and climaxed, spilling his seed.

Eleven

Even without an alarm clock, Luke awakened before dawn. He sat up and watched Maggie sleep. He thought she looked damn good in his bed. Night-tousled hair tangled around her face, and a pale-blue blanket covered her nakedness.

Smoothing her hair, he kissed her forehead. She made an incoherent sound and turned onto her side. He smiled, leaving her alone. She wasn't a morning person, that much he already knew.

Luke went about his usual routine. He washed his face, brushed his teeth, pulled on a gray sweatsuit and headed to the wet bar, grateful the suite provided an array of caffeine choices, including a no-frills brand of American coffee.

After putting on a pair of running shoes, he took his coffee onto the balcony, then sat at the glass-topped table and waited for the sun to rise, enjoying a misty view of the private beach.

Finding comfort in the wind and sea, Luke sat for hours,

studying the sky. Glittering beams of red and gold broke through the clouds, finally introducing the Mediterranean sun.

"I thought I'd find you out here."

He turned to see Maggie wrapped in a white silk robe, her eyes still sleepy, her hair tousled. She came toward him and when she leaned against the balcony rail, he caught the faint outline of her naked body beneath the thin material.

She looked enchanting as ever. A muse who inspired the arts—poetry, dance and song. She inspired lust, too, he thought. Fantasies he couldn't seem to control.

His sex stirred. "I want you," he said. "Right here. Right now."

"Do you?" She sent him a sultry smile and opened her palm. A foil packet shimmered in her hand. "I had the same idea, only I came prepared."

Reaching for her, he pulled her onto his lap and kissed her hard and quick. She tasted like mint, as cool and refreshing as the morning air.

She opened her robe and brought his head to her breast. He licked her nipples, then caught one with his teeth and tugged, just a little, just enough to make her moan.

Sliding his hands down her body, he caressed every curve, stroking her belly. She squirmed, and he moved lower.

When he plunged a finger deep inside, she gasped. She was wet and slick and eager. While the ocean rolled quietly upon the shore and clouds floated softly across the sky, Luke and Maggie went crazy.

She streaked up his sweatshirt to scrape her nails across his chest; he bit her neck and sucked the tender spot like a vampire.

He couldn't think, but he didn't want to. She was naked and straddling his lap, her white robe billowing like wings. All that mattered was her. Tasting, feeling, living out the lust.

He lifted his hips and tugged down his sweats. The moment he was free, the very instant the male hardness nudged her thigh, she tore into the condom, slipped it on him and sank onto his length.

He closed his eyes, and she rode him until he thought he might die—from beauty, from bliss, from emotions that slammed into his soul.

Her climax triggered his, and they shared a mind-blowing release, kissing and panting.

When it ended, when he could breathe again, he opened his eyes and knew he would never be the same. Not from the sex, but from her. She'd changed something inside him, and because he wasn't quite sure what it was, he told himself not to panic.

He wasn't going to marry her.

Pulling himself back to reality, he adjusted his sweats, feeling a bit awkward about removing the condom. "I hate these damn things."

She belted her robe. "I'll get on the Pill. I've taken it before."

During her affair with Claudio, he supposed. Luke didn't argue. He wanted the opportunity to spill inside her and not have to worry about conception.

If he wasn't going to marry her, then they weren't going to have children.

They went back to his suite. He discarded the condom, then resisted the urge to pace, recalling the night she'd asked him to come over and make a baby. He'd actually been tempted then.

And damn it, he was tempted now. He wanted to claim her, plant the seed of life so she would be connected to him forever.

Yet the idea of being a husband and father scared him senseless.

"Should I order breakfast?" she asked.

"Not for me." He knelt to tighten his shoelaces. "I'm going for a run." Something he did every morning before he showered. He wasn't avoiding her purposely, but today of all days he needed to clear his mind, to stop thinking about a commitment he didn't intend to make.

"Will you take Bruno along? He's probably anxious to get out."

"Sure."

Maggie opened the door to her suite and called the dog. The loyal mastiff appeared instantaneously. She patted the canine bodyguard and then gave Luke a gentle, heart-stirring kiss.

"I'll wait to eat until you get back," she said.

"Okay," he responded, trying to sound casual, even though his mind was still spinning.

Luke retrieved Bruno's leash and turned away. And with the dog by his side, he headed for the beach, wishing the Connellys' youngest daughter hadn't dared him to marry her.

The following afternoon Maggie and Luke interviewed Princess Catherine, gathering information about Gregor Paulus. They'd chosen to conduct the meeting in a relaxed environment, so they sat on a redwood deck at Dunemere that provided a soothing view of the sea.

Luke drank coffee, while Maggie and Princess Catherine sipped chamomile tea sweetened with honey. A platter of blueberry scones went untouched.

Studying Catherine with an appreciative eye, Maggie noticed changes in the other woman. Emotional changes that made the young princess more beautiful than she already was.

Love, Maggie decided, had given her feisty, headstrong cousin a graceful air of contentment. The dashing sheikh, Kajal bin Russard, she had married was truly her soul mate.

The way Luke is mine, Maggie thought, glancing at her lover.

"Was Gregor Paulus your father's confidant?" he asked the princess.

"Yes. Gregor was quite devoted to my father."

"So Prince Marc would have entrusted him with just about anything?"

She nodded, placing her tea back on the table. "Yes, I believe so."

"Will you tell me what you think of Paulus?" he asked.

"Truthfully, I don't like him." A strand of Catherine's auburn hair lifted in the wind. "Not in the least," she added, intensifying her statement. "When I was a child, he did his quiet best to diminish me in my father's eyes."

Maggie suspected that Prince Marc had been too self-involved to notice.

"And now?" Luke asked. "How does Paulus treat you now?"

"He tried to manipulate me soon after my father was killed. I was supposed to go out on the boat that day, but I couldn't make it, so Father took my place." She paused to sip her tea, to breathe a gust of sea air. "Gregor preyed on my guilt. He made certain that I knew he felt the prince died because of me."

"Bastard," Luke muttered.

"Quite," the princess agreed before he could apologize for the profanity. "But I don't allow Gregor to intimidate me anymore. These days he keeps his distance."

"Thank you for your time. I know how difficult all of

this has been for you," Luke said. "But I have one more question. Can you tell me why Prince Marc was driving the king's speedboat? Particularly since he wasn't originally scheduled to be on it that day?"

"King Thomas preferred to have someone else in the family drive. Because he was getting on in years and his eyesight was failing, he didn't take the boat out by himself anymore. But that wasn't something that was widely known."

"So you were going to pilot the boat before your father stepped in?"

"Yes. And I'm sure you can see how Gregor used that against me."

A short time later Maggie escorted her cousin to the limousine that waited to take her back to the palace.

They hugged and then looked into each other's eyes. There wasn't much more to say. Princess Catherine had been informed of her father's treachery, and she was coping with the knowledge, leaning on the man she loved for support.

Maggie returned to Luke and found him standing on the deck, gazing at the ocean, his hands thrust in his pockets, his jacket billowing in the breeze. She wished that he would lean on her for support, that he would trust her to help him trap Gregor Paulus.

"Prince Marc was a weak man," he said without turning.

She stepped closer. "Yes, he was."

Luke still watched the sea, concentrating, it seemed, on the rise and fall of each wave. "Which is exactly why he relied on someone like Paulus."

"You have a theory, don't you?"

"Yeah." He finally turned, his hair falling onto his forehead. "I think Paulus pulled Prince Marc into this."

''How? Marc is the one who had an association with the mob.''

''True, but I suspect that it was Paulus's idea to approach the Kellys about pirating those files from the Institute.''

''How?'' she asked again. ''Paulus couldn't have known about the cancer virus.''

''Marc probably told him about it when it first happened. And later, when Marc told Paulus that he was in trouble with the mob, Paulus devised a plan to appease the Kellys and get the prince out of hot water.''

Maggie sighed. ''And Marc went along with it because he was too spineless to face the Kellys on his own.''

''Exactly. He let Paulus do his dirty work for him.''

She met Luke's gaze, determined to convince him to allow her to help. Gregor Paulus was a force to be reckoned with, but with a carefully developed plan, she knew she could trap him. ''You have to let me—''

''No!'' He cut her off before she could finish her plea. ''You're not going undercover. Do you hear me? You're not.''

''Why are you being so stubborn about this? All I'm asking for is a chance to approach Paulus. I'll wear a wire, and you can be somewhere nearby, just in case there's trouble. And on top of that, I'll keep Bruno with me.'' Who in their right mind would try to hurt her with a two-hundred-pound mastiff by her side? ''Why do I have a canine bodyguard if I can't use him?''

Luke glared at her. ''Paulus is severely allergic to dogs. There's no damn way he would have a reasonable conversation with you if Bruno were there. And I'm not going to be listening with an earpiece while the woman I'm sleeping with is risking her neck. Let it go, Maggie. It isn't going to happen.''

At a standoff, they stared at each other. With her temper

flaring, she shot poisoned darts from her eyes to his. She ought to defy Luke and go after Paulus on her own. Prove to the stubborn detective that she was capable of much more than he'd given her credit for.

"Don't even think about it," he said.

"I don't know what you mean," she retorted.

"The hell you don't. It's written all over your face."

As a strand of her hair blew against her cheek, she shoved it away. Deep down, she knew that trapping Paulus without Luke's help would be next to impossible, but she had the right to fantasize about it, to imagine herself glorifying in personal triumph.

"I'm keeping my eye on you, Maggie."

Fine, she thought. If he was going to watch her like a hawk, then she would use this to her advantage and spend every waking hour right under his suspicious nose, concentrating all of her energy on winning the marriage dare.

She was mad as hell, but she still wanted to be Lucas Starwind's wife. She couldn't help it if she'd fallen in love with a macho, overly protective jerk.

After an exceptionally long, invigorating shower, Luke stepped out of the stall and wrapped a towel around his waist. Maggie sat at the vanity mirror, wearing a terry-cloth robe and applying her makeup. Apparently she'd bathed in her own suite, then moved all of her creams, lotions and cosmetics onto his countertop.

"What are you doing?" he asked.

"Getting ready." She stretched her eye, lined it with a creamy brown pencil, then smudged the line with a cotton swab.

He moved toward one of the double sinks. "Why didn't you finish getting ready in your own bathroom? Why'd you haul your stuff over here?"

"Because I'm moving in." She turned to face him. "I don't understand why we need two suites. We're sleeping together now."

But that wasn't the same as living together, he thought. Watching her settle into his domain made him feel as if they were in a committed relationship. Or, heaven help him, married.

"Your family is arriving tomorrow," he said. "And I don't think it would be proper to share a room while they're here."

Her jaw dropped, and she looked at him at if he'd just sprouted gills and a tail. "Good grief, Luke. My family isn't from the Dark Ages."

"You're still their baby." And he was the older man who ravished her every night, who couldn't seem to get his fill.

"We're consenting adults," she countered. "And being up front about what's going on is certainly more mature than sneaking into each other's beds. Besides, my parents are staying at the palace."

But some of her brothers and sisters intended to stay at the beach house. Her *married* siblings, he realized. Every damn one of them had settled down. In fact, Maggie was the last unmarried Connelly.

Preparing to shave, he lathered his face, frowning into the mirror.

"So, what's the verdict?" she asked.

He contemplated their situation further, scraping a disposable razor across his jaw. "We're keeping both rooms. I can't sleep with you while your family is here. It just isn't right. We'll have to learn to behave ourselves."

Maggie raised her eyebrows. "No wild moans in the middle of the night? No more early-morning romps on the balcony? I don't think that's possible."

He looked at her, and after several seconds of complete silence, they both burst out laughing. Wild moans. Early-morning romps. He supposed they did have the tendency to get carried away.

"Come on, Luke. Don't be so old-fashioned about this," she said when their laughter faded. "Let's move in together."

"I can't do that. Not in good conscience." Even if her family suspected that they were lovers, he wanted them to know that he wasn't using her, that his feelings for her were based on more than just sex. "This is my way of respecting you, Maggie. Please don't take that away from me."

"Oh." Her voice went soft, her eyes glassy. He could see that he'd touched her heart.

"So, will you work with me on this?" he asked.

She nodded, and he knew that if his face wasn't covered in shaving cream, she would have kissed him.

"I promise to behave," she said. "But I'm not giving you up after this trip is over."

"I know." They would remain lovers for a while, he thought. But it wouldn't last forever.

Luke returned to the mirror and finished shaving, looking forward to a night on the town. Maggie had offered to take him on a tour of Altaria, treating him to her favorite places.

He drove the European SUV they'd rented, and she gave him directions, guiding him down narrow roads flanked with cobblestoned sidewalks and buildings rife with old-world charm.

They stopped at a quaint little café, and Luke allowed Maggie to order, then wondered what he'd gotten himself into when the appetizer was served. The marinated olives and zucchini seemed normal enough, but he refused to try the stuffed squid, eyeing the suction cups with displeasure.

Maggie tossed her head and laughed, and he knew she'd ordered it to tease him. Where food was concerned, he wasn't nearly as adventurous as she was.

On an outdoor, heated patio, they drank Chianti and talked, their conversation as vibrant as the wine.

Luke studied his companion. Her hair, loose and straight, fell past her shoulders. She wore slim-fitting jeans and a denim blouse. Her buckskin jacket was smooth and feminine. Beautiful, he thought. *Bella,* just like the Italian waiter had called her.

Their entrées arrived, and they dined on eggplant, roast chicken and potatoes seasoned with mouthwatering spices. Luke wanted to lean across the table and kiss Maggie, but decided that dragging his sleeve through a side dish of pasta wasn't the most gentlemanly way to steal a kiss.

After their meal, he took advantage of the opportunity to touch her. They strolled, hand in hand, down imperfect sidewalks, stepping over cracks and chips in the stone. Stars lit up the night, the Big Dipper pouring silver specks across a royal-blue sky.

Maggie guided Luke into an ice-cream parlor. They ordered two melon sorbets, then resumed their walk, eating the refreshing dessert along the way.

"What do you think of Altaria?" she asked.

He finished his sorbet. "I love it." And he loved this moment, this carefree evening with her.

"Let's go there," she said, indicating something across the street. "I've always wanted to see what it was like."

He turned, expecting an old stone church or another historic building. But instead she pointed to a magic shop, a tiny establishment with ancient symbols on the door.

Healing crystals dangled from serpentine chains, and candles flickered, sending jasmine-scented smoke through the air. An older woman with long gray hair and watchful eyes hovered near a glass case. The proprietor, Luke thought. A local Gypsy who probably read tea leaves and tarot cards.

He met the old woman's gaze, and suddenly his breath lodged in his throat. He could feel her power, the energy that flowed through her veins.

And because he was a superstitious man, a Cherokee who knew magic existed, he tried to break eye contact, but found himself trapped.

She removed a tiny glass figurine and handed it to him. ''Terpsichore,'' she said. ''The muse of dance.''

He glanced at the fragile glass figure. The goddess held a gold lyre, and on her head she wore a crown of leaves.

''Terpsichore knows what's in your heart,'' the old woman said.

A qua da nv do. My heart.

He'd lost his heart the first time he'd danced with Maggie, and now the Gypsy wanted him to admit that he'd never gotten it back, that Maggie, his muse, had claimed it for good.

I don't need this, he thought. I don't need someone prying into my mind. Or trying to convince me that I'm falling in love.

He handed the figure back to her, but she refused to accept it. ''Keep it,'' she said, turning away from him.

Feeling unsteady, Luke considered leaving the muse on the counter, but quickly changed his mind. He didn't know anything about the old woman's culture, but in his, it was rude to refuse a gift.

Unsure of what else to do, he headed straight out the door, leaned against the building and pulled a much-needed gust of air into his lungs.

"What was that all about?" Maggie asked, rushing after him.

"I don't know," he lied, even though the tiny muse glowed in his hand.

Later that night Maggie sat next to Luke on his sofa, a pillow between them. Her family would be arriving tomorrow morning, which meant she wouldn't be seeing much of Luke, and just the thought alone made her miss him.

But worse yet was his detached behavior. She feared he was reverting to his reclusive self. He seemed disturbed by the incident with the Gypsy. Maggie didn't understand why, and he hadn't offered an explanation.

"What did you do with the muse?" she prodded, moving the pillow.

He motioned to the bedroom. "It's on the dresser."

"I wonder why the Gypsy gave it to you."

He shrugged. "I have no idea."

She studied his profile. A golden light from the fire bathed his skin, intensifying the razor-edged slant of his cheekbones and strong, determined cut of his jaw. "Did you even know who Terpsichore was before the Gypsy mentioned her?"

"Sort of. I knew that there were nine muses, and that they were goddesses from Greek mythology, but I didn't know their names."

"Pegasus was from Greek mythology, too," she said, thinking about Gwen's winged horse. "In fact, when Pegasus was a colt, the goddess Athena entrusted the muses with his care."

"I know." He turned to look at her. "Pegasus was so excited to meet the muses that he struck the side of Mount Helicon with his hooves and caused two springs to gush forth. Springs of inspiration or something."

Maggie nodded. Luke seemed to know the story quite well. "Did you read to Gwen about Pegasus?"

"My mom did. But I always thought the idea of a winged horse was pretty cool, so I paid attention, too."

Now Maggie understood. The muse figurine probably reminded him of Gwen. And that was why the Gypsy's unusual gift had unnerved him. "So many mystical things have happened," she said. "I painted Gwen without knowing it, and now the Gypsy gives you a muse. All of this must mean something."

"I don't know. I guess. I'm trying not to make a big deal out of it."

"Don't be sad, Luke. I think Gwen is watching over you. Like an angel."

He met her gaze, his dark eyes suddenly struck with emotion. "Thank you," he whispered. "That was a nice thing to say."

She reached for him, and they embraced. And because she felt his heart pounding next to hers, she shivered. She wanted to tell him that she loved him, but she wasn't sure if this was the right time.

Maggie drew a nervous breath. This had to be the right time. Once her family arrived, she wouldn't get the chance. There would be no more stolen moments, no more candlelit dinners or romantic strolls on the beach.

Luke would probably spend his days discussing the sting operation with Rafe. And while they were devising a plan for an undercover agent to trap Paulus, she would be busy with her sisters.

No, she thought, there would be no time for confessions of love.

Luke nuzzled her neck, and she felt her pulse quicken.

"There's something I need to tell you," she said softly.

He ended their embrace. "What is it?"

She looked right at him. "I love you. And not just as a friend. I love you the way a wife loves a husband."

He went perfectly still, and when he finally spoke, his voice sounded raw. "You just think you do. What you're experiencing is some sort of youthful infatuation."

Hurt, she squared her shoulders, preparing to defend herself. "Please don't talk to me like I'm a fickle-hearted teenager. I'm a grown woman. And I love you, whether you believe it or not."

He shook his head. "I don't believe it."

Drawing strength from her pride, she did her damnedest to keep her eyes dry. She wouldn't cry in front of him. Not now. "Why would I have dared you to marry me? Why would I have offered you that kind of commitment?"

"Because you *think* you love me. You're confused."

"Damn you." Her temper rose, and unable to stop the blast of anger, she socked his arm. The least he could do was acknowledge how she felt. "You're a jerk, you know that?"

He grabbed her wrists before she could pummel him again. And then he straddled her, pinning her to the couch. "I have no idea what in the hell to do about you, Maggie. You're driving me crazy."

You could love me back, she wanted to say. You could open your stubborn heart.

They stared at each other, and for a moment she thought that he might kiss her, that his frustration might turn to passion. Or, she prayed, to an admission of love.

But it didn't.

Breaking eye contact, he released her. "Go back to your own room, Maggie. Get some sleep and forget about this."

"You're asking me to forget about the way I feel? To convince myself that I don't love you?"

"Yes," he said. "I am."

Twelve

The Connelly siblings weren't a quiet bunch. They were, in Luke's opinion, an interesting gene pool sired by Maggie's father, Grant.

Three out of the eight boys had been conceived with women other than Maggie's mother, Emma. Thirty-six-year-old twins, Chance and Douglas, sons Grant hadn't been aware of until this year, were products of a relationship he'd had before he'd married Emma. Thirty-two-year-old Seth, on the other hand, had been produced from an affair Grant had had with his secretary while his marriage to Emma had been on shaky ground.

Grant and Emma, now completely loyal to each other, weren't staying at the beach house, but there were enough Connelly heirs present to keep Luke's head spinning. Through the lively conversation and rustle of linen napkins, no one seemed to notice Luke's discomfort. He sat at the cherry-wood table, doing his damnedest to dodge eye contact with six-year-old Amanda, or Mandy, as she was often called.

The child watched him, and he didn't know why. Luke couldn't read kids. He'd spent a lifetime analyzing his peers, yet children managed to elude him. But as far as he could tell, Mandy was the apple of her daddy's eye and quite enamored of Kristina, the woman twenty-seven-year-old Drew Connelly had married.

"Where's Aunt Maggie?" the little girl asked Luke.

He finally turned and met Mandy's curious gaze. "She's in her room. She isn't feeling well." Or more than likely, he thought, she was avoiding him.

"What's wrong with her?"

"She has a headache."

"Did she take some aspirin?"

"Yeah, I suppose she did."

A maid served their salads, and Luke breathed a sigh of relief. Mandy would be too busy eating to chat.

Serving bowls of ranch dressing were passed around the table. After Mandy doused her salad, Luke accepted the dressing, poured some onto his greens and then handed it to Seth, who thanked him with a polite nod.

Luke considered Seth the black sheep of the family. His mother, Angie Donahue, the secretary Grant had dallied with, had turned Seth over to Grant and Emma when he was a hard-edged, scrappy twelve-year-old. Unable to control the wild youth, they'd shipped him off to military school, where he'd learned to distance himself from his prominent family.

But these days, Luke noticed, Seth seemed right at home with the Connelly clan. He'd overcome plenty, including the heart-wrenching knowledge that his mother had come back into his life for the sole purpose of aiding the Kelly crime family in the smuggling scam.

As Luke picked up his fork and concentrated on his salad,

Seth leaned toward his wife, Lynn. They bent their heads together like the newlyweds they were.

Damn it. There were too many married couples at the table, he thought. Too many happy, madly-in-love Connellys.

"How come you're frowning?"

Luke turned to see Mandy, her head tilted, white-blond bangs dusting observant green eyes.

"I wasn't frowning. I was eating."

"Nuh-uh. You were making a face like this." She furrowed her brow and turned down her lips, exaggerating a bitter scowl.

He wondered if he looked that surly all the time. "I guess I've got some things on my mind."

"What?" she asked.

"Nothing that concerns you," he responded.

"Grown-ups always say stuff like that." Quite properly, she adjusted the napkin on her lap. "But they don't fool me. I'll bet you had a fight with Aunt Maggie. You probably gave her a headache."

At this point, Luke decided that Miss Mandy was six going on forty. "You're pretty smart for a kid." And he was a first-rate heel. He'd hurt Maggie's feelings last night, refusing to believe that what she felt for him was real.

But he didn't want her to be in love with him. Nor did he want to face the fact that he might be falling in love, too.

"I saw you dancing with her," Mandy said.

His chest constricted. Terpsichore. The muse of dance. "You did?"

She nodded. "At Uncle Rafe's wedding. I could tell she liked you. I was going to help you guys be together, but my dad and Kristina said I already did enough matchmaking. They got married because of me."

He couldn't help but smile. Amanda Connelly was an angel, an adorable little girl with invisible wings.

Don't be sad, Luke. I think Gwen is watching over you. Like an angel.

Maybe she was, he thought as Mandy grinned at him. Maybe she was.

After dinner, Luke went into the kitchen and asked the maid if she would prepare a plate for him to take to Maggie.

He carried the tray upstairs and received a boy-has-our-little-sister-got-you-whipped look from three of Maggie's brothers. In return, he sent the Connelly men a hard stare. Single guys were supposed to rib married ones, not the other way around. But that hadn't stopped Rafe, Seth and Drew from chuckling.

Luke knocked on Maggie's door—the door in the hallway rather than the one that connected their rooms.

She answered, clearly surprised to see him. She wore a satin robe, and her hair was coiled into a hasty topknot, damp tendrils falling from the confinement. She smelled like sunshine on a breezy, winter day.

"I thought maybe you could use a little food," he said.

"I was going to order something later."

"Oh, well...I can take this back." He shifted uncomfortably, picturing himself passing her brothers again.

"No. That's okay. You can come in."

He entered her room and set the tray on a nearby table. "How's your head?"

"Better, thank you."

Because he didn't know what else to do with his hands, he shoved them in his pockets. Her nipples were hard. He could see them pearling against the satin robe. He suspected that she'd just stepped out of the tub, which accounted for the flowery scent clinging to her skin.

"Is something on your mind, Luke?"

"No. I just stopped by to bring you dinner." And to tell her that she'd healed a deep and painful part of him. Although he would never forget what had happened to his sister, Maggie had helped him see Gwen as an angel rather than the victim of a violent crime.

But now that he was here, preparing to talk to Maggie, he couldn't form the words, fearing they would lead to another discussion—one he wasn't ready to confront.

Love. Marriage. Babies.

Luke was still afraid of making that kind of soul-searching commitment, especially with Maggie. He didn't trust her reckless spirit, the youth and the vigor that made her who she was.

She drove him crazy with worry. What if she tried to go after Paulus on her own? He knew damn well that the thought had crossed her mind.

"I want a promise from you," he said. "A solemn vow."

She searched his gaze. "What?"

"That you'll stay away from Paulus."

Her shoulders tensed. "We've already established the fact that I'm not getting involved in the sting operation." She looked him directly in the eye. "But if you want a vow, then you've got it. I'll stay away from Paulus."

"Okay." He backed off, but she was still meeting him eye to eye.

"It's your turn," she said. "To promise that you won't try to end the marriage dare before New Year's Eve."

He expelled the air in his lungs. The sheers that draped the sliding glass doors were open. Beyond the balcony, the moon lit the beach in a golden hue. He imagined watching her dance on the shore, her robe billowing, her hair catching the moonlight.

His mermaid. His muse.

"I promise," he said, before turning away from the wonder of the sea and the woman who seemed to be part of it. The woman he couldn't get off his mind.

On the morning of the coronation rehearsal, Maggie wore an elegant apricot-colored dress, spun from the finest silk and accented with a strand of pearls. She was, after all, the daughter of a former princess and the sister of the soon-to-be-crowned king. And today she knew she must look and behave the part.

Gazing at her reflection, she debated on how to style her hair. Should she wear it loose or work it into a French twist?

Maybe something in between, she thought as she pulled it back with a rare, jeweled barrette. Preparing for the long day ahead, she slipped on a pair of low-heeled pumps, then walked onto the balcony and let the ocean breeze caress her face.

And then she saw Luke, exercising the dog. They'd just completed their daily run and were headed toward the house. They made a striking pair—the powerful warrior with his copper skin and raven hair, and the loyal mastiff with his fawn-colored coat and dark, masked face.

Suddenly Luke stopped and glanced up. Did he sense she was there? Did he know she had been watching him?

Everything seemed so uncertain now. She'd admitted that she loved him, and he'd agreed to go on with the dare, yet they engaged in awkward glances and strained conversations.

Even with the distance between them, their eyes met, and she knew he would wait for her on the deck. Strained conversations or not, he wanted to talk, to warn her to be careful at the rehearsal.

She sighed and turned away. She wished he trusted her instincts. At times he made her feel like a child.

Maggie went downstairs and caught the aroma of coffee

brewing and bacon frying. Breakfast, she assumed, would be served shortly. She passed two of her brothers on her way outside. They sat in the living room, a newspaper divided between them, both men attired in dark suits. The entire Rosemere-Connelly family would be attending the coronation rehearsal today. And on the afternoon of the actual event, each would hold an esteemed seat in La Cattedrale Grande, the Altarian Grand Cathedral.

Maggie walked onto the redwood deck and caught sight of Luke.

"Hi," he said. "You look incredible."

"Thank you."

He looked incredible, too, but she doubted he would believe her if she told him. Sweat beaded his forehead, and his hair, tousled from the wind, shone with blue-black highlights.

Luke shifted his stance. "I wish you would agree to take Bruno with you today."

Maggie glanced at the mastiff. Bodyguard or not, it didn't seem appropriate to bring a dog to the cathedral. "I'll be fine. My family will be there."

"Don't go anywhere alone," he persisted. "Not even for a second."

"I won't."

"Not just at the cathedral, but at the palace, too."

"Please. Stop worrying. King Daniel and his queen have been living at the palace for nearly a year. My parents are staying there, not to mention Princess Catherine and Sheikh Kaj. And of course there's my sister Alexandra and her husband, Prince Phillip." She paused to finger her pearls. "Paulus isn't going to blow his cover with everyone around."

"I know. I just wanted to warn you to be careful anyway."

Would he worry at the coronation, too? she wondered.

Or would he feel differently because he would be attending that event? Maybe Gregor Paulus and his accomplices would be caught by then. She certainly hoped so.

"Have some faith in me, Luke. I won't do anything to get Paulus's attention. In fact, I probably won't even see him." She envisioned a long, formal day saturated with Altarian protocol, something most of the Connelly heirs and their spouses were still learning. "If anything, wish me luck. You know how I tend to forget my manners." And royal manners, in her opinion, were staid and tedious.

Luke grinned, and she envied his leisure day. Aside from the presence of a nonintrusive domestic staff, he and Bruno would have the beach house to themselves.

"Good luck," he said, still smiling.

And what a smile, she thought. All those straight white teeth flashing against bronzed skin. "How about going for a midnight stroll with me tonight? We can count the stars." And steal a passionate kiss beneath a bright, crescent moon.

"That sounds nice. I've missed you, baby."

A tingle warmed her spine. "Me, too."

He pulled a hand through his hair. "I better catch a shower before breakfast. I can't come to the table like this."

All rugged and gorgeous. She couldn't imagine why not. Watching him go, she wished she could stay home with him.

And make love until they both ached for more.

As expected, the coronation rehearsal had been long and exhausting, but awe-inspiring, too. Maggie looked forward to the upcoming ceremony, imagining her brother taking an oath to govern the people of Altaria. She could already see him, kneeling at the altar, strong and handsome in the commander-in-chief uniform that came with the responsibility of the throne.

But for now His Majesty had arranged for a small, private banquet at the palace for the Rosemeres and the Connellys.

Maggie sat at the end of the table, next to her sister, Tara, who had been reunited with her long-lost husband, Michael Paige, a man who had once been presumed dead. The Rosemeres and the Connellys had suffered through tragedies and prevailed in triumphs, and Maggie was proud to be a member of both prestigious families.

The conversation was warm and friendly, but by the time Maggie finished a bowl of chilled pumpkin soup, her tenderhearted mood turned to disorientation. Suddenly she felt ill.

Drawing a deep breath, she lifted her water, then took a small, careful sip. Had the spicy soup disagreed with her? Or had it been the stuffed grape leaves and the shrimp dumpling appetizers?

Somehow that didn't seem possible. Maggie was accustomed to rich, elaborate foods. Then what was wrong?

She frowned at her empty bowl. Maybe she was coming down with the flu.

Not now, she thought. And not here. The last thing she wanted to do was spoil the beauty of this intimate dinner.

But a wave of dizziness had set in. The room was blurring, the unicorn tapestries melting off the walls, horns and hooves bleeding into the carpet.

She turned to her sister. "I'm not feeling very well."

Tara reached for her arm. "Do you want me to walk you to the nearest powder room?"

"Please."

With Tara hovering like a mother hen, Maggie sat on a velvet sofa in the ladies' lounge and cursed her body for failing her. She rarely took ill. Although she'd had a headache yesterday, she'd attributed it to stress. "I think I caught a virus," she told her sister.

"Oh, my," Tara said before she turned and asked the powder-room attendant to bring Maggie a moist cloth.

The middle-aged woman returned with the cloth. As Maggie dampened her face, she looked up at Tara, feeling guilty for taking her sister away from the banquet. It wasn't often the entire family spent an evening together. "Go back to the table and finish your meal."

"I'm not leaving you here."

"Please. I'll be fine. I just need to rest."

The powder-room attendant turned to Tara. "Excuse me for interrupting, ma'am. But if Miss Connelly would like to go home, I can call for a palace chauffeur."

"What do you think, Maggie?" her sister asked. "Do you want to return to Dunemere?"

"Maybe. I don't know. Just let me sit here for a while."

Although it took some prodding, Maggie finally convinced Tara to finish her meal. After all, she wasn't completely alone. The powder-room attendant was there.

"I'm coming back to check on you," her sister warned. "And I'm bringing Mother and Alexandra."

Wonderful, Maggie thought. If she vomited, the women in her family would be in attendance. Oh, yes. This was truly a royal affair.

After Tara left, Maggie closed her eyes and willed the queasiness to settle.

"The nausea will pass," she heard the powder-room attendant say, as if her mind had just been read. "But you will experience dizziness, blurred vision and drowsiness. Eventually, you will sleep."

Stunned, Maggie opened her eyes. The dark-haired lady sat in a nearby chair and clasped her hands on her lap, her demeanor suddenly changed. Maggie's stomach rolled. Catching her breath, she met the other woman's gaze, realizing the brunette worked for Paulus. "My food was drugged."

"Yes. When your sister returns, you'll tell her that you want to go home, and you sent me to fetch a guard. And so your family doesn't worry, the guard will escort you to one of the palace limousines with instructions for the driver to take you to Dunemere."

"But that isn't where I'll be going? Is it?" Paulus wouldn't send her home to Luke. "Where's Lucas Starwind? What have you done with him?"

"He hasn't been harmed. Yet," the phony attendant said in a cold voice. "But if you don't cooperate, Mr. Starwind will be killed."

Dear God. *Luke.*

Confused and dizzy, Maggie struggled to think, to reason. Why was she being kidnapped? For ransom? Or was Paulus going to use her as a bargaining tool, demanding exemption?

She balled the damp cloth in her hand. Did it matter? Eventually her family would discover she was missing, and the king would do what he could to save her. But if she alerted her family now, Luke wouldn't stand a chance. The man she loved would be murdered.

"I'll cooperate," she said, her voice raw, her pulse pounding.

The other woman nodded, and when Maggie's mother and sisters came to check on her, she told them that she wanted to return to the beach house. Her mother tried to convince her to lie down in a guest room in the palace, but Maggie insisted on going to Dunemere. She would feel more comfortable in her own bed, she lied, and she'd already called ahead to tell Luke to expect her.

Luke, she thought. Her lover, her heart—the man they might kill.

Five minutes later Maggie went willingly with the Royal Guard, knowing the impostor was an accomplice in her kidnapping. And as she climbed into the car that was waiting to take her to an unknown destination, she prayed Luke was safe.

Luke stepped onto the boardwalk with Bruno by his side. He'd received an anonymous phone call instructing him to go to the pier. The caller had claimed that he had pertinent information regarding the Connelly case.

He stopped at the rail and faced the ocean as he had been instructed to do. His instincts told him that something was terribly wrong, and for that reason he'd brought the dog.

Death, he thought, clung to the air, like salt from the sea. He gave Bruno a command that told the dog to watch for suspicious strangers. If someone intended to plug Luke in the back, Bruno would alarm him first.

His senses keen and alert, he gazed out at the ocean, at the water that sloshed in dark, ominous waves. The 9mm he wore clipped to his belt had become an extension of his body, and on a night such as this he wouldn't hesitate to use it.

If someone was going to die, it sure as hell wasn't going to be him.

Hesitant footsteps sounded, and Bruno growled deep in his throat. The footsteps paused, and then a masculine voice came out of the night. "Call off the dog."

Not on your life, Luke thought. Giving Bruno the command to wait for further instruction, he turned to view his opponent.

The other man stood tall and thin, a long, hooded coat draping his lean form. Luke knew it was Gregor Paulus.

The edge of the pier they dominated was isolated, with

streaks and shadows dancing across the boardwalk from the wind.

Luke moved closer, and both men faced each other. The glow from the lampposts cast a buttery light, making Paulus appear gaunt.

"You have information for me?" Luke asked.

"Yes." Paulus's features distorted, and Luke suspected the breeze had carried Bruno's scent to his nostrils, irritating his allergies. "Maggie Connelly has been abducted, and she won't be returned until you uncover a document proving that Rowan Neville is the Kelly crime family's Altarian contact."

The impact of Paulus's statement slammed into Luke with the force of a Mack truck. But years of covert military operations and private investigations kept him steady.

"How will I uncover this document?"

"It will be provided for you within two days. And at that time you will shift the focus of your investigation, clearing my name and framing Rowan Neville."

"What happens to Maggie?"

"You will be contacted and given the location of where you can find her. But only after you interrogate the security chief and claim that he admitted to the wrongdoings, including Miss Connelly's kidnapping." Paulus squinted and sniffed. "You will tell the Connellys that Rowan Neville panicked, fearing that you didn't believe the lies he'd told you about his children being threatened."

Luke imagined lunging at the other man and ripping his heart out, then tossing the bloodied organ into the sea, feeding the sharks. "How did you take Maggie away from her family without their knowledge?"

The royal aide detailed the abduction, pride sounding in his nasal, allergy-irritated voice. "Of course, once the family returns to Dunemere to ask you how Miss Connelly is faring from her illness, you will have to tell them that you haven't seen her. This will cause a panic, no doubt. Which means you must play your part, Mr. Starwind. The heroic lover who will go to the ends of the earth to find his woman. And put her kidnappers behind bars.''

''Am I supposed to clear Rocky Palermo, too?'' Luke asked, knowing that Rocky held Maggie captive somewhere.

''Yes. Although it's a known fact that Mr. Palermo is associated with the Kellys, he wasn't part of this particular operation. The hit man who aided Neville is Edwin Tefteller, the one Rafe Connelly captured in Chicago last month.'' He paused to dab his nose with a handkerchief. ''When all of this is over, I'll resign from the royal service, and both Mr. Palermo and I will disappear quietly. You'll never hear from either one of us again.''

Luke pictured Rocky's hard, brutal face. ''If Maggie is harmed in any way, if that son of a bitch touches one hair on her head, I'll come after you and Palermo. And I'll torture both of you until you moan for mercy like the cowards you are.''

''There's no need to get testy.'' The other man stepped back as Bruno growled again. ''As long as you and that beast,'' he added, including the dog in his summary, ''are willing to cooperate, Miss Connelly won't be harmed. But if you make one false move, your lovely lady is dead.''

A shiver knifed Luke's spine. He knew that meant Rocky was waiting for word from Paulus on the outcome of this meeting. ''I'll cooperate.''

''Very well.'' The royal aide had the gall to smile. ''It's been a pleasure doing business with you, sir. But I must return to the palace. I intend to be there when the king learns that his sister is missing. I am sure that he, like the rest of the Rosemere-Connelly family, will be devastated.''

Gregor Paulus turned and walked away, but Luke knew he had to let him go. Maggie's life depended on it.

The building was dim, and the faint, scattered security lights that shone on the machinery made the hulking pieces look like monsters with ill-shaped heads and gnarled teeth.

Bound and gagged, Maggie sat on a cold concrete floor, frightened and confused. The drug made her head fuzzy, and her eyes wouldn't focus. She thought she knew where she had been taken, but she wasn't sure.

Refusing to sleep, she battled the drowsiness she'd been told to expect. How long would she be kept here? And when would Paulus make his demands?

She tried to swallow, but the gag limited the movement. Her mouth ached, and her throat felt parched. As her eyes watered, she thought about Luke. Was he being kept somewhere nearby? Had they drugged him, too? And how had they gotten past Bruno? Had they killed her dog?

Footsteps sounded, and she cringed. She saw her captor's hazy figure approach, so she closed her eyes, feigning sleep and praying that he would leave her alone. Even in her confusion, she knew who he was.

Thirteen

Luke knew exactly what he had to do.

He had to find Maggie.

Tonight.

He couldn't leave her alone and frightened, just as he couldn't betray the Connellys and allow Paulus and his accomplices to go free.

Still standing on the pier, he checked his watch. How much time did he have before another man or woman joined Rocky Palermo? Before the security on Maggie tightened? An hour? Two if he was lucky?

Because Paulus had been vain enough to detail the kidnapping, Luke figured out how many players were involved. Besides Rocky Palermo, it was possible four others had pulled this off: the attendant in the ladies' lounge, the kitchen maid who'd drugged Maggie's food, the man who'd impersonated a palace guard and the phony limo driver who'd taken her to a preconceived location—the place where Rocky would be.

Luke suspected the guard and the limo driver were the masked computer hackers Rowan Neville had told him about. But he wasn't sure who the women were. He hadn't counted on females being part of Paulus's operation.

Bruno looked up at him, and he reached down to touch the dog. "I didn't keep Maggie safe," he said to the mastiff. Just as he hadn't kept Gwen safe.

As an image of his sister's kidnapping surfaced, Luke willed it away. He wouldn't let guilt distract him from this mission. Gwen was dead, but he wasn't going to lose Maggie. With Bruno's help, he would rescue her and bring her home.

Home. To his arms. His bed. His life.

Don't, he told himself. Don't fall apart. Don't slide into the despair of surviving without her, into the gut-wrenching fear that they will kill her just to spite you. He knew emotional agony would only trip him up, and he couldn't afford any mistakes.

He had to focus, not with his heart, but with his head, with the cognitive skills that made him an effective investigator, a civilian soldier.

But the only way to do that was to tap into his enemy's mind. To think like Paulus, to become him for an instant in time.

With the wind blowing and the sea crashing in black waves, Luke closed his eyes.

Gregor Paulus was a man who had chosen to hide in plain sight. He'd kidnapped Maggie from a heavily secured palace, thumbing his nose at the royal family in the process.

Where would a man like that take a captive?

Somewhere familiar. Somewhere that gave him a sense of power.

Luke opened his eyes, and suddenly he knew. The textile mill. Paulus and Cyrus Koresh, the now-deceased owner, had been comrades, and Paulus probably still had a key.

It made perfect sense. Particularly since the mill was closed for several weeks and wouldn't reopen until Koresh's brother flew in from France to sell a business he'd inherited but didn't want.

The textile mill produced a variety of goods, and that meant the building was filled with various types of machinery, including enormous looms and vats for dying yarn.

Maggie could be hidden anywhere in the factory, if she was truly there at all. Luke paused at an employee entrance. He didn't have time to disengage a sophisticated alarm system, but there was a good possibility that it wasn't activated.

Taking a chance, he broke into the building. Silence greeted him, and he welcomed the sound of nothingness. Drawing his gun, he sent the dog a few paces ahead. Bruno knew Maggie's scent.

They crept through the mill, taking to the shadows. The factory seemed ominous at night, dimly lit and foreboding. A huge, circular machine that knit yarn into fabric could have easily spun a web.

Bruno stopped, and Luke took heed. A bullet of adrenaline shot through his veins. Maggie was near. But so was Rocky.

In the next second he saw a figure cross their path. A man, broad and muscular, a gun in his hand.

Inhaling a steady breath, he watched Rocky pace. Back and forth. Agitated. Impatient. Waiting for reinforcements.

Dream on, you son of a bitch, Luke thought as he gave Bruno a command. Trained to kill, to protect its master at all costs, the mastiff lunged before Rocky knew what hit him.

Struck with fear, Palermo lost his weapon in the battle.

And as he lay on the ground with the snarling dog's jaw attached to his neck, Luke knelt beside him.

"If you so much as bat an eyelash, my friend here is going to rip out your throat," he warned in a low, vile whisper. "So if I were you, I wouldn't move a muscle."

With that said, Luke picked up the hit man's gun and went to Maggie.

And suddenly the emotion he'd been banking flooded his system. Bound and gagged, she sat on the floor in her silk dress and pearls, tears streaming down her face.

His Maggie. His muse. Dear God, what had they done to her?

He removed the gag, and she gulped a breath. "I thought you had been captured, too," she said. "I was so afraid. That woman said they would kill you. Oh, Luke, is it really you? Please tell me I'm not dreaming."

"It's me, baby. Everything's going to be okay." He untied her wrists, and went to work on her ankles. He had to move fast, but he wanted to stop and caress her, to hold her and never let go. "One of the other men might be on his way here," he told her. "I have to call the palace and inform the king."

He made the call on his cell phone, then used the gag and ropes on Palermo, wishing he could let the dog rip him to shreds instead. With Bruno's help, he forced the muscle-bound hit man into the back seat. The mastiff took control of the prisoner, snarling in Rocky's face.

Next, Luke scooped Maggie into his arms, and she put her head on his shoulder. She looked so pale, so tired and weak.

"They drugged me," she said.

"I know." He carried her out of the building, put her in the passenger's seat and drove directly to the hospital, where armed guards handpicked by the king would be waiting.

* * *

Maggie slept in a hospital bed while Luke kept vigil in a nearby chair. Throughout the evening, concerned family members had filtered in and out of the private room after presenting proper identification to one of the Royal Guard stationed outside Maggie's door. She would suffer no ill effects from her ordeal, at least not physically. But Luke worried about her emotional state.

He'd been given clearance to stay the night, but he'd refused the blanket the nurse had offered him. He didn't want to sleep. He wanted to be aware of Maggie, to see the rise and fall of each breath she took, to listen to the little sighs she made while she dreamed. Restless dreams, he noticed. Her subconscious mind was troubled.

The door creaked open, and Luke reached for his gun. Who would come into the room at four in the morning?

He saw the trusted guard and relaxed.

"Rafe Connelly is here. He wants to see you."

"Send him in," Luke responded.

Rafe looked exhausted. He'd stopped by a few times earlier, but now the shadows under his eyes had darkened. Luke supposed his own face was just as drawn. Adrenaline, fear and Lord only knew how many cups of vending-machine coffee weren't a healthy combination.

"How's she holding up?" Rafe asked about his youngest sister.

"Still sleeping. But that's good. The doctor said she needs the rest." Because the room was dim, illuminated by only a soft night-light, Luke squinted. But in spite of the hazy glow, he knew the circles under Rafe's eyes weren't an illusion. Nothing about this night had been conjured by sleight of hand, mirrors or magic. Every heart-pounding hour had been real.

"I came by to tell you that it's over." Rafe moved closer,

his footsteps deliberately light. "Paulus and his team are in prison. The Royal Guard caught every last one of them."

Luke released a heavy sigh, the burden of fear lifted. They couldn't go after Maggie now. She was truly safe. "Who were the women?"

"The powder-room attendant was a member of the Kelly crime family we didn't know about, but the kitchen maid was actually a true employee with the royal service staff. She was Paulus's secret lover. They'd gone to great lengths to conceal their relationship."

"And the phony guard and limo driver were the Altarian computer hackers who'd stolen the files?"

Rafe nodded. "The limo driver told us where the rest of the CDs are being stored. He seems to think the police will go easy on him because he didn't kill anyone." A small smile tugged at his lips. "For being a technical wizard, he isn't too bright."

Luke smiled, too. And then he watched Rafe walk toward Maggie and stand beside her bed.

"My sister went willingly with the kidnappers," Rafe said, his voice barely above a whisper. "She jeopardized her own life because she thought yours was in danger."

Luke's heart clenched. "I know."

"She loves you, Starwind."

Another clench. Another emotional pull that had his heart aching. "I know that, too." And he loved her, as well. He'd been in denial all this time, but he couldn't lie to himself any longer. Maggie had been living inside him since the moment he'd danced with her at Rafe's wedding reception.

The other man met his gaze, and for a moment they stared at each other. The look that passed between them said it all. The case was over. Maggie no longer required Luke's protection. What she needed from him went much deeper.

Rafe slipped quietly out of the room, and Luke knew he was headed to Dunemere to be with Charlotte, his new wife.

For the next two hours, Luke resumed his vigil in the straight-back chair, and when dawn broke, Maggie stirred.

"Luke?" She said his name softly, and he went to the side of her bed.

"I'm here, baby." He smoothed a strand of hair from her cheek. She looked sleepy, but not nearly as pale as she had been earlier.

She gazed at him with blue-green eyes. "Why am I still in the hospital?"

"The doctor wanted to keep you overnight for observation. I'm sure he'll release you later today." To ease her mind, he told her that Paulus and the others had been caught. "It's over. No one is going to hurt you ever again."

"You saved me," she whispered, giving him a look so tender, it made his knees go weak.

"Bruno helped. I couldn't have done it without him."

"Can I keep him, Luke? Will his trainer sell him to me?" She adjusted her position in bed. "I can't bear to give him back."

"I'll call his trainer today." And do whatever it took to make sure Maggie and Bruno remained together.

The mist of morning streamed into the room, and Luke and Maggie sat quietly for a short time. He still had fears, insecurities that he was too old to start a family with her. She was still in grad school. A lifetime still spanned between them. He hoped and prayed that loving her was enough.

"Christmas is just a few days away," she said.

"Yeah. It really snuck up on us, didn't it?"

She smiled. "We've been kind of busy." Thoughtful, she fingered a strand of hair. "Do you think we could go back to Chicago for Christmas? I'd like to see how your mother is doing, and I need to get away from here for a little while. Just a short break before the coronation.''

''Sure.'' He wanted to spend the holiday with her, snuggled in front of the tree he'd decorated. ''I think it's snowing back home.''

''Good.'' She smiled again, and he knew his heart would never be the same.

On Christmas Day, Luke's town house smelled like roast turkey, corn bread stuffing, cranberry sauce, mashed potatoes and pumpkin pie. Nell and Dana had cooked and brought the traditional meal, and now the holiday was winding down, with both women preparing to leave.

Maggie reached out to hug Luke's mother. This was the first time Dana had been to her son's home. Although she hadn't been taking her antidepressant long enough to benefit from its full effect, the medication appeared to be helping. She'd panicked a little on the long, congested drive, but once she and Nell had arrived, she was thrilled to spend the day in Chicago—a city she hadn't seen in twenty-seven years.

''Are you going to be okay on the way home?'' Maggie asked.

Dana exhaled a deep breath. ''I don't like all that rush-rush traffic, but I should be all right. And if I get too nervous, I can always take the tranquilizer the doctor gave me. He discouraged me from using them too often, but he thought I might feel better knowing they're available.''

''Luke and I are proud of you.''

''Thank you. It actually feels good to get out. And to see the two of you together,'' she added in a soft whisper.

Maggie squeezed Dana's hand. Luke had been open with his affection in front of his family, and Dana and Nell had noticed every tender kiss and warm gesture. But in spite of his loving behavior, he'd yet to say the words. He was still holding back, and Maggie didn't know why.

"We better get going," Nell put in. "It'd be best to get home before dark."

Another round of hugs was exchanged. Maggie waited at the door while Luke walked the women to their car and made them promise to call as soon as they arrived at the farm.

A light coat of snow blanketed the ground, and holiday lights twinkled as far as the eye could see. It felt good to be home, Maggie thought. But it worried her, too. The case was solved, and her life would resume in Chicago. But how long Luke would be a part of it, she couldn't say. He hadn't mentioned the marriage dare or what the outcome would be.

Luke came back and took Maggie's hand, then guided her to the sofa. The Cherokee tree, as she called it, glimmered with lights and Indian jewels. Strands of turquoise beads draped each branch, and leather-wrapped feathers made an earthly statement.

"I have another gift for you," he said.

"You do?" They'd already exchanged a bundle of presents with his family.

"Yeah. But I have a question first. How many children do you want?"

Caught off guard, she blinked. "I'm not sure. Two, maybe three." Her heart fluttered right along with her lashes. "Are you offering to give me a baby? Is that my gift?"

"Yes. No. Sort of." He couldn't seem to get the words right. "This is…I'm…" He paused, leaving the sentence dangling. "I figured you'd want to finish grad school before you had kids."

She decided not to comment on his assumption since she

wasn't quite sure where this conversation was leading. "I'm confused, Luke. What's going on?"

He reached into his jacket pocket and produced a ring-size box. "I've been carrying this around all day." Flipping open the top, he presented her with a marquise-cut diamond that blazed like a star.

A rapid pulse burst through her body. "Oh. Oh, my." It was beautiful. Dazzling. And completely unexpected.

"I'm asking you to marry me. And have my children. But I was hoping that you didn't want to wait too many years before we started having kids, because I'm not getting any younger. I'll be old and gray before you know it."

And that, she realized, was why he'd been holding back.

He glanced down at the ring, then back up at her. "I love you, Maggie, and I know you love me. And I apologize if this isn't a very romantic proposal. But I need to know that you're going into this with your eyes open. I'm nearly forty years old, and you're still in your early twenties."

"My eyes are open." And she was staring right at him, memorizing every rawboned feature in her mind. "We don't have to rush through our lives, worrying about our age difference. We'll live each day as if it's our last. We'll enjoy every moment, and we'll have babies when the time feels right." She slid a hand into his hair. "You're going to make an incredible father, whether our first child arrives next year or three years after that."

He leaned forward and brushed his lips across hers. "My beautiful, free-spirited Maggie. Do you know why the Gypsy gave me a muse? Because she could read my mind, and she knew that I'd fallen in love with you the first time we danced."

Her eyes watered, misting with tears.

"*A qua da nv do.* It means my heart. And that's what you are." He took the ring and slid it on her finger. "When

Paulus told me that they'd kidnapped you, I forced myself to stay strong. But deep down, I was afraid they'd kill you just to take you away from me.'' He paused, his voice rough with emotion. ''I couldn't have survived without you, Maggie. My heart would have died.''

''We're fine. We're both fine.'' She couldn't stop the tears from falling. ''And we're going to be together for the rest of our lives.''

''Promise?'' he asked.

She nodded and crossed her heart, then placed her hand over his. It thumped against her palm, strong and steady. With lights blinking on the tree and ice fogging the windows, she unbuttoned his shirt. She would never forget this glorious Christmas Day.

He scooped her up and carried her to his room. The four-poster bed was carved from a rich, masculine mahogany, and his sheets rivaled the color of grapes turning sweet and dark on the vine. Maggie tasted his lips, the potency of his kiss.

They took their time undressing each other, hands questing. She knew he loved her. Not because he'd told her, but because she could feel it in his touch.

He fanned her hair around the pillow, slid his palms over her skin, following the curve of her body, molding her, claiming her as his own.

''You healed me,'' he said. ''You won the dare.''

''Because you let it happen. A part of you wanted to be healed.''

He lowered his head and ran his tongue over her nipples, sending delicious little flutters low in her belly.

''You bewitched me, Maggie. You bewitch me now.''

The playful licks turned to a deep, hard suckling. Reaching for the bedpost, she moaned and arched, thrilling him.

She could feel his fire, the heat and the hunger, the scorching contact of mouth against breast.

Intent on giving pleasure, he moved lower. It was exquisite torture. Tender yet somehow edged with talons, with the promise of a hot, explosive climax.

He dipped his tongue into her navel, and her stomach jumped. But as he trailed that warm, wet mouth over her thigh, her entire body convulsed, anticipating more. So much more.

In one quick motion, he lifted her hips. "My beautiful Maggie. I can't get enough of you."

She slid her hands into his hair, and he kissed between her legs. Kissed until her breath sobbed and her soul quaked.

Chips of cedar burned in a clay pot, and the diamond on her finger flashed like lightning, a streak of white blazing in the wood-smoked room. She gripped the bedpost for support and let him push her over the edge.

And when her heartbeat stabilized and her breath returned in gasping pants, she saw adoration shining in his eyes.

"Luke." With sighs and strokes, she enticed him to join with her.

Anxious and aroused, he made a low, primal sound and covered her body with his. She held him close, soothing his desire, taming the urgency.

Maggie wanted this feeling to last.

He caressed her cheek; she pressed her forehead to his and cherished the man she would marry. And then they made love.

Slow and easy, yet brimming with passion.

They moved in unison, dancers lost in each other's eyes. Images of winter sweetness filled her mind, like honey swirling and spinning, then melting over snow-kissed skin. And it would always be this way, she thought as his heart took hers.

This feeling was hers to keep.

Always and forever.

Days later Luke and Maggie returned to Altaria, but this time they shared a suite at Dunemere. Bruno had spent Christmas with the royal family, being pampered at the palace, but now he was back at the private beach with Luke and Maggie.

After a vigorous run along the shore, Luke showered, shaved, dried his hair and then proceeded to attire himself in a black tuxedo.

Maggie stood at a full-length mirror, putting the finishing touches on her appearance. Her satin dress, the color of the moon and sprinkled with sequins that could have been stars, flowed to the floor like a December rain, reflecting glints of light. Her hair was swept away from her face and pinned into an elegant twist. Iridescent pearls rested at her neck and adorned her ears. A pair of gauntlet gloves and satin pumps completed the stunning ensemble.

Luke had to remind himself to breathe. He loved her beyond reason, this woman who had healed his heart.

Suddenly he had the urge to unzip her dress, slide his hands through her properly coiffed hair and pull her onto the canopied bed in a flurry of white satin and floral-scented skin. Love, he thought, moving toward her, was a powerful emotion.

And so, heaven help him, was lust.

Aware of the desire brewing in his loins, she met his eyes in the mirror. "Don't you dare, Lucas."

He grinned, knowing full well that he had to behave. "Can't a guy fantasize around here?"

She turned, running her gaze quite deliberately over him. "Maybe I'll indulge in a little fantasy myself. You look dashing, Mr. Starwind."

"Thank you, Miss Connelly."

"I have something for you." She went to the dresser and opened a jewelry box. Producing a small diamond earring, she held it up for his inspection.

Luke smiled. He knew his pierced ear fascinated her. He removed the tiny silver hoop he always wore and let her slip the diamond in place. The faceted stone winked against his dark skin.

"Perfect," she said, brushing his lips with a tempting kiss.

He tasted her lipstick and went after her tongue, doing his damnedest not to mar her exquisite image. A long, black limousine was already waiting to take them to the cathedral.

She kissed him back, refreshed her lipstick and promised to indulge his fantasies when they returned from the ball tonight.

He intended to hold her to that promise, knowing she wore a mouthwatering bustier, adjustable garters, thigh-high hose and a pair of sheer lace panties under her dress.

A few minutes later Luke escorted Maggie to the car. This afternoon the Royal Bishop, Altaria's religious head of state, would minister King Daniel's coronation.

When Luke and Maggie arrived, they followed the lavish procession and took their designated seats. A provision had been made for Luke to remain by Maggie's side during the ceremony. Although he wasn't part of the Rosemere-Connelly family yet, his engagement to Maggie was official, the ring on her finger a testimony of love and commitment.

Awed by his surroundings, Luke studied the opulent inlay and marble columns stationed between carved archways and colorful mosaics.

Clearly, the Grand Cathedral lived up to its name. The remarkable medieval structure, built of high-quality stone, had withstood the ravages of time. And because ancient architecture fascinated Luke, he knew many of the original stones contained masons' marks, signs and symbols denoting the early craftsmanship. The mark befitting the ceremony today was called the Sign of Honor, a symbol that transformed into a crest—a coat of arms incised on the stones.

King Daniel's sword, sheathed at his side, bore that very crest. Standing at the front of the cathedral, he wore the impressive armed forces uniform Altaria bestowed upon its commander-in-chief. A blue sash spanned his chest, and gold braiding trimmed a doubled-breasted jacket decorated with medals, ribbons and gilded buttons.

The ceremony began with the Royal Bishop addressing the people in attendance. As the bishop spoke, the young king faced his subjects.

"I present unto you King Daniel, your undisputed king. For all of you who come this day, he offers homage and service. Are you willing to do the same?"

In one clear voice of acceptance, the people responded, "God save King Daniel!" and a shiver raced up Luke's spine.

The king turned and knelt at the altar, waiting for the bishop. The holy man then administered the coronation oath.

"Sir, is Your Majesty willing to take the oath?"

"I am willing," the king said.

Luke listened while Maggie's oldest brother placed his hand upon the Bible and swore to govern the people of Altaria according to the country's laws and customs. He completed the oath by saying, "These things which I have promised, I will perform with honor. So help me God."

As the coronation robes were draped around King Daniel's broad shoulders and the crown centered upon his head, Luke held his breath and Maggie's eyes filled with tears. The Imperial Crown, encrusted with priceless jewels and enhanced by the kaleidoscopic light from a stained-glass window, shone like a beacon of authority.

The king bowed his head in prayer, and those assembled did the same, humbling themselves to the Creator above and beseeching His guidance for the rest of their days.

It was, Luke thought as he closed his eyes, a moment he would never forget.

The magnificent stone castle had impressed dukes, duchesses, lords, ladies and heads of state who'd been invited to lavish balls over the centuries, and this celebration was no exception.

The Emerald Ballroom housed an exquisite dining room and generous dance floor, where modern renovations blended with the mystique of medieval architecture.

Malachite floors swept the interior in polished splendor, offering swirling shades of green. Light spilled from crystal chandeliers, pouring over the grand hall like a fountain. Twisted columns shimmered with gilded inlay, and circular tables were set with fine linens, indigenous floral arrangements and bone china bearing the royal crest.

The Connelly family sat with the king and queen in the center of the dining room. King Daniel looked strong and handsome in his uniform, and Queen Erin, a former royal protocol instructor and the lovely woman Daniel had married, dazzled the eye in a stunning gold gown and diamond tiara.

Maggie's entire family was present, each adding their own special flair to the gathering. It was, she thought, the most glorious affair she had ever attended.

Queen Erin had selected the menu, choosing recipes from around the globe. The appetizers, prepared by a renowned chef, tempted the palate with a variety of international flavors. The crispy artichoke flowers hailed from Italy, and the crab and coconut dip boasted Caribbean roots.

Yes, Maggie thought, everything was perfect. While she enjoyed truffled quail eggs and caviar moons, Luke favored sweet-corn flans, an appetizer that probably reminded him of a Cherokee dish. Corn, she knew, was a staple in his heritage.

She turned to smile at him—her lover, her warrior, the man who had risked his life to save hers.

He returned her smile, letting her know how pleased he was with the choices they had made. Because Maggie wanted the opportunity to plan the wedding of her dreams, they'd decided to marry the following year. And in the meantime, they'd agreed to divide their time between Maggie's downtown loft and a country home Luke intended to buy, where the richness of the land would soothe his Cherokee soul.

While Maggie studied her fiancé, he leaned toward Mandy Connelly. The six-year-old sat beside him in a taffeta gown and jeweled barrettes, looking like a fairy-tale princess with white-blond hair and sparkling green eyes. Maggie knew Luke had bonded with her niece, and seeing them together warmed her heart.

"Will you save a dance for me?" he asked the child.

"Yes, thank you, sir," she responded, her royal manners intact. Mandy was a precocious girl who could wrap a man around her little finger and tie him in a loving bow. Clearly, Luke had been knotted nice and tight.

Mandy's father, Drew, touched her shoulder. He was the man she had practiced that perfect little bow on. "Should we make our announcement?" he asked her.

The child glanced at Kristina, her adoring stepmother. They exchanged a knowing smile, and Mandy took the helm. Tapping on her water glass, she got the attention of everyone at the table with a delicate crystal chime.

"My dad and Kristina are going to have a baby," she said, flashing a sister-in-waiting grin.

"Two babies," Drew put in as he nuzzled his wife and winked at his daughter. "Twins."

The Connelly family erupted in joy. The king proposed a toast and flutes were lifted in celebration. Luke clinked Maggie's glass, and they smiled at each other.

"Do you think that could happen to us?" he asked.

She knew he meant the arrival of two babies at once. "I don't know." She glanced at Drew, who shared a toast with his twin, Brett. Her brothers were lucky to have each other. "I hope so."

"Me, too," Luke said.

Touched, she brushed his cheek with a gentle kiss, then noticed her father watching them.

Grant Connelly, attired in a traditional tuxedo and diamond cuff links, sat next to his bejeweled wife, beaming with pride. All of his children had found love and happiness. No one in the family was immune, including Maggie's cousin, Princess Catherine, who dined with Sheikh Kaj at her side.

Nearly two hours later, the six-course meal ended in a decadent dessert, a cognac trifle garnished with sugared cranberries and mint leaves.

As Maggie dipped into the custard and cake, Luke sipped a cup of black coffee. "Can you imagine how they must feel," he said, referring to the king and queen. "Knowing their firstborn son will rule a nation someday?"

Maggie smiled, realizing Luke was still thinking about procreation. "It must be an incredible feeling," she agreed as the king reached for the queen's hand.

The royal couple danced the first waltz, the picture of

grace and elegance. Soon other couples joined them, and the ballroom came alive with music and regal splendor.

"Would you like to dance?" Luke asked.

Emotional and misty-eyed, Maggie nodded. Moments later, as they glided eloquently across the floor, the rest of the world disappeared. Suddenly they were the only two people on earth.

She gazed into his eyes. "It's just like before." They had fallen in love the first time they'd danced, and on this magical evening, they were falling in love all over again.

"You really are my muse," he whispered. "My heart. My inspiration."

Lost in each other, they stepped onto the balcony. Beyond the castle, stars lit up the night, and the scent of winter flowers bloomed in the air.

As Luke lowered his head to kiss her, Maggie closed her eyes, knowing a Cherokee angel named Lady Guinevere rode across the sky on a winged horse, granting dreams, wishes and marriage dares meant to come true.

*   *   *   *   *

DYNASTIES: THE CONNELLYS

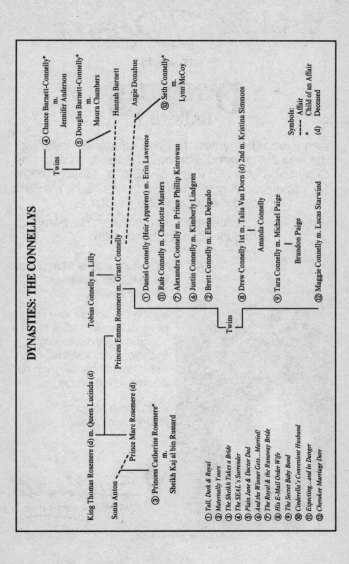

King Thomas Rosemere (d) m. Queen Lucinda (d)

Sonia Anton

Prince Marc Rosemere (d)

Tobias Connelly m. Lilly

Princess Emma Rosemere m. Grant Connelly

Twins
④ Chance Barnett-Connelly*
m.
Jennifer Anderson

⑤ Douglas Barnett-Connelly*
m.
Maura Chambers

Hannah Barnett

Angie Donahue

③ Princess Catherine Rosemere*
m.
Sheikh Kaj al bin Russard

① Daniel Connelly (Heir Apparent) m. Erin Lawrence

⑪ Rafe Connelly m. Charlotte Masters

⑦ Alexandra Connelly m. Prince Phillip Kinrowan

⑥ Justin Connelly m. Kimberly Lindgren

② Brett Connelly m. Elena Delgado

⑧ Drew Connelly 1st m. Talia Van Dorn (d) 2nd m. Kristina Simmons

Amanda Connelly

⑨ Tara Connelly m. Michael Paige

Brandon Paige

⑫ Maggie Connelly m. Lucas Starwind

⑩ Seth Connelly*
m.
Lynn McCoy

Twins

Symbols:
- - - - - Affair
* Child of an Affair
(d) Deceased

① *Tall, Dark & Royal*
② *Maternally Yours*
③ *The Sheikh Takes a Bride*
④ *The SEAL's Surrender*
⑤ *Plain Jane & Doctor Dad*
⑥ *And the Winner Gets...Married!*
⑦ *The Royal & the Runaway Bride*
⑧ *His E-Mail Order Wife*
⑨ *The Secret Baby Bond*
⑩ *Cinderella's Convenient Husband*
⑪ *Expecting...and In Danger*
⑫ *Cherokee Marriage Dare*

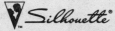

COMING NEXT MONTH

#1483 THE PLAYBOY & PLAIN JANE—Leanne Banks
Dynasties: The Barones
Gail Fenton was immediately attracted to her boss, gorgeous Nicholas Barone, but she assumed he was out of her league. Then suddenly Nicholas seemed to take a much more *personal* interest in her. Was she wrong, or had this Cinderella finally found her prince?

#1484 BECKETT'S CONVENIENT BRIDE—Dixie Browning
Beckett's Fortune
While recovering from an injury, police detective Carson Beckett tracked down Kit Chandler Dixon in order to repay an old family debt. But he got more than he bargained for: beautiful Kit had witnessed a murder, and now she was in danger. As he fought to keep her safe, Beckett realized he, too, was in danger—of falling head over heels for sassy Kit....

#1485 THE SHEIKH'S BIDDING—Kristi Gold
The Bridal Bid
Andrea Hamilton and Sheikh Samir Yaman hadn't seen one another for years, but one look and Andrea knew the undeniable chemistry was still there. Samir needed a place to stay, and Andrea had room at her farm. But opening her home—and heart—to Samir could prove very perilous indeed, especially now that she had their son to consider.

#1486 THE RANCHER, THE BABY & THE NANNY—Sara Orwig
Stallion Pass
After he was given custody of his baby niece, daredevil Wyatt Sawyer hired Grace Talmadge as a nanny. Being in close quarters with conservative-but-sexy-as-sin Grace was driving Wyatt crazy. He didn't want to fight the attraction raging between them, but could he convince Grace to take a chance on love with a wild cowboy like himself?

#1487 QUADE: THE IRRESISTIBLE ONE—Bronwyn Jameson
Chantal Goodwin knew she was in trouble the minute Cameron Quade, the object of her first teenage crush, strolled back into town. Quade was the same, only sexier, and after what was supposed to be a one-night stand, Chantal found herself yearning for something much more *permanent!*

#1488 THE HEART OF A COWBOY—Charlene Sands
Case Jarrett was determined to honor his late brother's request to watch out for his widow and unborn child. The truth was, he'd secretly loved Sarah Jarrett for years. But there was a problem: She didn't trust him. Case knew Sarah *wanted* him, but he had to prove to her that her fragile heart was safe in his hands.

SDCNM1202